Fault Zone:
Diverge

An Anthology
by the
San Francisco/Peninsula Writers Club
© 2015

Fault Zone: Diverge is the fifth anthology of short stories and poems produced by the San Francisco/Peninsula Writers.

SHRP
Sand Hill Review Press

Introduction

Just about the time we were finishing up copy editing for *Fault Zone: Diverge,* a 6.0 earthquake hit Napa, California. Thankfully, there was no loss of life, but damage in the city of Napa was extensive and it was the largest magnitude quake in the area in a quarter century.

The quake—like other unexpected events—reminded me how quickly our actual and imagined futures can diverge.

Many of the stories, essays, and poems in this volume of *Fault Zone* feature individuals whose lives turn out quite differently than they had imagined. Whether walking in spirals in a labyrinth by the sea, looking back on a summer spent in a hosiery factory, or serving up revenge with a side of cappuccino, these characters take us with them on their sometimes circuitous but always entertaining journeys.

I'm often surprised when a group of stories, presumably submitted by people who have not consorted with one another before submitting, end up with thematic similarities. The civil rights era forms the backdrop of several pieces in this volume. Some of the poems are deeply personal; others are broadly political. There's love and heartbreak and the humor inherent in being a parent.

So prepare to travel down a different path than the one you might have expected as you embark on reading this, the fifth edition of the *Fault Zone* anthology series.

Thank you to all the writers who submitted to this edition, whether your work was selected or not. We pay homage to your continuing efforts. It's not easy to get up and write day after day, month after month, year after year. It's even harder to open yourself up to others by sharing what you write.

Thanks to our use of the Submittable online submission system, we were able to keep track of manuscripts and authors far more easily than in the past. Fortunately, the automation does not extend to the selection process. That's still done by real human beings. Thanks to Dorcas Cheng-Tozun and Lisa Meltzer Penn, who weighed in when Assistant Editor Linda Okerland and I needed a third opinion. Dorcas and Lisa, along with Katherine Gerster, assisted with copy editing. And thanks to Laurel Anne Hill, our manuscript proofreader, who reviewed the entire manuscript to check for typos and out-of-place commas before we went to print.

Thanks also to San Francisco/Peninsula Writers, a branch of the California Writers Club, for bringing together a fabulous group of writers every month and providing us a community in which to hone our craft.

I hope you travel your path with joy and anticipation, however divergent it may be.

Audrey Kalman, Editor
San Mateo, California

Table of Contents

Fault Zone: *Diverge*

Audrey Kalman, Editor
Linda Okerlund, Assistant Editor

To the Labyrinth
By Diane Lee Moomey

AFTER A NIGHT OF WIND AND RAIN, you will wake early with a question that has puzzled you for years. Never before has it been so clear. You will pick up the car keys and, barely dressed, go out without coffee.

You will drive north beside the western ocean, approaching El Granada, to a beach recommended by a good friend. When you look seaward you will notice a large white ball perched on a bluff, and think: *I do not want to go there.* You do. You will drive further, to a traffic light, to a road leading into the harbor. The marina will be on your left, and on your right a mall with large restaurant. The street ahead will be lined with more restaurants and a hotel. Again you will think *I do not want to go there.* You still do.

Past the restaurants, the hotel and the brewing house, you will turn left by the Mezza Luna and drive to the T. You will turn right and then left. Or left and then right—either choice will carry you past the welders, the storage companies, the yacht club, the boats in dry dock and the sellers of anchors and surfing supplies. At the end of that street, you will turn right and pass a lumberyard, then follow a line of yellow posts as they curve through small hillocks of chaparral.

For the first time today you will know *I do want to go there.*

The pavement curves past coyote brush and cattails until the road itself offers you a choice: either bear right and continue up the last hill to the white ball, or turn left onto dirt. On this day you will turn left, leaving your car alongside many others. When you see a black retriever fastidiously picking his way between puddles, you will start walking.

You will continue southeast along a dirt road with the salt marsh on your left side and an upslope on the right. (If you doubt these directions, any of the ducks can point you straight.) Past the egrets you will come to the sailboats at anchor. The labyrinth—you have heard tales of these—will be on your left. You may think to go there straightaway, but that would be a mistake. It is best to walk on as if you did not notice this labyrinth, as if you are determined to reach the ocean, so you can catch it unawares on the way back.

Past the catamaran is the jetty. You will stand on that for awhile, with the wild sea to your left and smooth water to your right, then walk north onto sand to the far end where the rocks are piled. The tide will be low, so you will sit on a black boulder and look out to sea, listening to your question.

At this point you will be ready for the labyrinth. You will retrace your path and find it now on your right.

Labyrinths there are which cannot be seen in one glance, whose curves cover the crests of hills, whose pattern is known only to their makers and to those gifted with flight. Labyrinths there are whose paths are hedged: green walls, where one walker cannot see another. Labyrinths there are which, if you did not have as much faith in their creators as you do, you would not dare enter.

This labyrinth is none of those. You will see its entirety in one glance, see every arm of the path outlined in small stones. Since last night's rain was heavy, some of those stones may have fallen out of place. You will listen again to your question, then enter on the downhill side walking with narrow stride. As you go along you will replace the tumbled stones.

Dogs will pass by and ask *what do you think you are doing by walking in spirals*? Do not answer them—they are only jealous because they did not think of this first. Their people will smile apologetically.

"I don't know where she gets these ideas," they will tell you.

You will come to the center and stand still for a moment, expecting something to happen. If others are waiting to enter you might feel uneasy, since this labyrinth is not wide enough for two walkers to pass. You will stay anyway, just for a moment. Your question will still be with you, though perhaps with less intensity than before. In time you will decide that nothing at all is happening, and will find your way back to the entrance, nod to the next person waiting, not look back as you walk to your car.

You will drive to Café Classique and order the Grande breakfast, which you rarely do. You will put a great deal of nutmeg and cream in your coffee, and although the wind is still cold will take all this outside to the table beneath the *Brugmansia*. You will arrange scrambled eggs into a small mountain with your fork, and fancy that one large orange blossom will fall upon your plate. One after another, you will dip fries into too much ketchup and eat them. This also, you rarely do.

After the eggs, after the fries with ketchup and the coffee with nutmeg, you will set down your fork. You will look up at the orange flowers, down at your plate and then as if from a great distance will see your question. From the couple at the next table, you will ask to borrow a pen. You will begin to write voluminously on paper napkins.

O Bind Not My Words in Paper Edges
A sestina
By Frank A. Saunders

Where in the seed is the scent of roses?
Why do you want to cage my meaning in a page
of paper, straight-cut, with edges that bring
uniformity to thoughts wanting to be free as air,
boundless as a roiling coil of smoke,
smoke that seeks to startle, alerting every nose?

Don't bind my book in hard-bound covers, where your nose
can never encounter the dried scent of page-pressed roses,
archiving it in parlors reeking of tobacco smoke,
with lemon-oil-soaked chairs, with tables devoid of any page
of reading matter, where the dormant air
has no living vibrancy to bring.

Shout these words with all your strength. Let your voice bring
a bracing call to the hearer, so he knows
that a new song, a new breeze stirs the air,
blowing out the dust of ages, bringing in the scent of roses
tinged with the acrid smell of blood, of hordes in full rampage
running closer, closer through the smoke

of turmoil. Can your voice pierce the pall of smoke
and fear that paralyzes us, we the speechless? Can you bring
a hint of hope that future writers can record a page
of history more peaceful, where every citizen knows
that, stronger than decay, a drop of oil of roses
can dispel the stench of cordite hanging in the air?

Even a simple spider, weaving a dew-jeweled web in the air
as dawn-warmed moisture rises from the ground like smoke,
feels a shiver as a bee, back from breakfasting on a bed of roses,
blunders into the sticky net, to bring
itself as breakfast, signaling to the quivering spider's nose
that food has arrived to sustain, in his life's book, another page.

So make haste to free the words imprisoned on this page.
Release their message to the shimmering air
for all to breathe, pointing a direction for each nose
to follow, pervading the universe like smoke.
Publish this score so that all the world may bring,
in singing, a worldwide harmony fragrant with roses.

Burn this page. Let its smoke
rise into the air and bring
to every nose the scent of roses.

The Feint of the Other Shoe
By Elise Frances Miller

ANNA LOWERED HERSELF ONTO A BAR stool at Bix
in North Beach. She held herself straight on the stool, feeling
the tight skirt of her new cocktail dress from Neiman Marcus
ride up above her knee at just the right angle. To Anna,
appearance was, as always, an integral part of the plan. The
goal was to solve the problem of loneliness while remaining
single. To become a *successful* lonely person. A titter rose
inside her, but she quashed it. At the Bix Bar, she supposed
she must look like an extremely wealthy hooker, like the
mistress of one of the Levi Strauss heirs or, God forbid,
Sheldon Adelson. She wrinkled her nose and, this time,
giggled out loud. Then, shaking off the moment with a deep
breath, she caught the bartender's eye.

Soon, with her classic martini in front of her, Anna felt
like she truly belonged at Bix. Hell, by the sheer size of her
expenditure at Neiman's, Saks, and the Maiden Lane
boutiques, she *absolutely* belonged at Bix. A jazz trio at the
end of the bar struck up something bland and retro. She
sipped and stirred her martini with the olive pick, leaning
into the gentle hum of well-heeled clients.

But when she swung around to face the trio, she hit her
designer Drakes against the peg leg of the barstool and felt
one heel scrape off and fall to the floor. *Shit*, she thought.
Second time that day with the Drakes. The first time she'd
stumbled over a break in the sidewalk. *What a klutz*, she
scolded herself. Now she was forced to climb back down,
awkward at best, retrieve the errant shoe, and remount.

She primped her hair. How she loved her hair. Nothing
mussed it. She could count on the long, thick, honey-brown
waves, a glitter-fuchsia stripe curling in front.

Again, she made sure the skirt hit just the right point,
and now checked that the hot-pink segments of her lace
bodice were positioned to reveal her cleavage—but, of
course, not too much of *that* candy.

She had been here before in the early days, on her nights off after working two or sometimes three jobs, then grinding concepts into her brain at the library in between. She had been such an anomaly: an undereducated, underfunded Jewish girl. Constantly analyzing how to get from *A* to *Z* with an alphabet missing a few letters. Surely this game could not be tougher than the ones she had played to make it in a city like San Francisco. Back then, Bix was just a place to observe and relax in the safety of the wealth net, dressed as well as she was able and sitting for a half hour as if she was waiting for a date. Later, she hung out in more affordable dives, preferring to test her new identity in a boisterous crowd where everyone was trying like blazes to stand out. When she was noticed on Columbus Avenue, she knew she had achieved the classy but original look she was after.

Even with her elegant hooker look and, at thirty-four, testing certain givens, she had calculated that the sparkling shades of pink and magenta, her defiant posture and ever-so-slight smile would scream above the ambient buzz for someone available to come take a chance.

The first gambler who sat down by her side was not the one she wanted. *Dammit.* He had the right suit—she would know the fit and texture of an Armani mohair wool when she saw it in any light, dim or harsh. Would have set him back two grand if he hadn't dressed himself secondhand, like she had in the early days. Made her speculate if he lived near her classy Marina condo or had maybe nabbed a place in one of those nifty new downtown high-rises.

It was his smile that didn't live up to expectations: crooked teeth, one in front jutting out and glinting in the pin light above the bar. His thin, gently curved nose and unruly hair thrust out at precisely the same concave angle as that tooth, as if everything about him was already grabbing at her. Anna's brain shifted to her library reading, to three arches over the neoclassical doorway. *Maybe*, she thought, if those teeth had been side-by-side and not plunging toward her.

All the same, his jaw was square and his flesh was clear and firm. A healthy guy, with that mop of hair balanced

15

midway between shoulders that had seen the inside of a gym. He ordered from the bartender. When he grinned again, Anna noticed his lopsided teeth were as white as a Colgate commercial. She pulled her face back down to her martini, then took a sip, hoping he hadn't noticed her staring.

To put herself at ease, and to move forward with her plan, she told him a little too loudly, "You've got a great smile. I'll bet you never had to live through braces in middle school." *So rude*, she thought, a martini-induced snigger trapped in her chest. She had to push him off that barstool, *n'est-ce pas*?

But life is full of surprises, and this guy had plans of his own. He held out his hand as politely as an Asian sales rep and said in a perfectly American way, "I'm glad you lived through braces yourself, because your smile is awesome. And, by the way, I'm Joe."

Wouldn't you know it? Joe, for heaven's sake. She had no option but to drop her hand into his. "Annabelle," she said, deciding at once that he would not have the satisfaction of her real name. But then the invisible force of her practiced self-determination took hold of her. She had a goal, after all. So she chuckled good-naturedly, looked into her lap and back up into his face, and said softly, "I'm sorry, but my real name isn't Annabelle, and I would appreciate it if you would move to another bar stool. This one is...reserved."

"Oh gee, sorry, you were waiting for someone?"

"Not exactly. Well, sort of."

Once again, on her way from *A* to *Z*, there was a gap at *J*. For Joe. He kept his eyes on Anna's for way too long to be natural. She maintained her composure, and finally he sighed and looked away. Then he spoke in the tone he should have used in the first place, Anna reflected, to ask if the goddamned bar stool was free.

"Excuse me, but are you a bigot?"

"A what?" she screeched and looked around to make sure the couple to the right of her situated their snoopy eyes back on their gross green gimlets. "No! No, I'm not a bigot," Anna replied with as much resentment as she could muster.

Her mind raced to protect her dignity, but all she came up with was, "I'm a Jew, for Christ's sake. Jews know how it is to be stung by that. I would never be a bigot."

Joe laughed and shook his head. Took a sip of his citrus vodka martini, as if it would calm some hilarity that Anna could not fathom. *What obscure ethnicity was he, anyway?* she wondered, rifling through her mental catalogue of Central European types. *Maybe Croatian? Or Bulgarian?*

She watched him polish off his cocktail—it looked more appetizing than her traditional martini. She had never thought to order something different. She wondered if his breath smelled like orange, lemon, grapefruit... Hell, what was she thinking? And, fuck it, he was not *going* anywhere. Finally, he spoke from some deep secret source of knowledge that, without knowing why, she trusted. "Jews can be on the receiving end, as I just felt I was," he said. "But they—I mean, we—can be as anti-Semitic as anyone else."

Now he had Anna's attention. "You're talking about self-hatred. And besides, I didn't even know you were Jewish. Never crossed my mind."

He snickered. "Like hell you didn't. Every American, Jewish or not, has known I was Jewish my whole life," he continued. There was less resentment in his voice than Anna would have expected. "American bigotry is sly. It tries, especially in big coastal cities, to be politically correct. Not to offend."

"But, then, I obviously intended to offend—and *gotcha.* You were offended, on cue."

"Yeah, I guess I was. Maybe it's your European background. Or else you're not from San Francisco. There was nothing oblique about your comment."

"I've been here for nearly fourteen years. And my family hasn't been in Europe for 150."

"And my family was on its way here from France about the same time," Joe said.

"France? Not the usual Polish and Russian background? How did that happen?"

"Have you ever heard about the slaughter in Paris in 1870, after the Franco-Prussian War? My ancestors evidently knew that where the Germans tread no good would follow, even then."

"But I know my history. The Germans didn't hurt the French as much as they hurt each other. And nobody was after the Jews."

"Well, it was Europe. So everybody was after the Jews at one time or another."

"And still are."

The two of them laughed their bitter laughs then. Anna hailed the bartender and pointed at Joe's citrus drink. "One of those, please."

Joe asked for a refill. With his face turned to order, his three hooks were not so prominent. *What an ugly* punim, Anna thought. And crap, she did not want a Jew. She was no bigot, but a Jew dating a Jew was a recipe for her parents' decades of *Sturm und Drang*. Memories flooded in of her stratagems for escape from her unbroken home—the one that should have been ripped apart by divorce before she'd had to endure all those years of screaming hatred, but never had been, even to this day.

No, thank you!

Frantically, she tried to think of some excuse to extricate herself. Maybe the ladies room, then just head out without saying good-bye. This couldn't be the first time someone cut out on poor Joe. But why was she thinking "poor Joe"? He was clearly successful at whatever he did. And he didn't seem as lonely as she felt at that moment, a big empty bubble opening up inside her chest. She wanted to stop feeling sorry for herself. She actually shook herself a little. *So, okay, he will be fine*, she thought. *I won't hurt his feelings if I take off.*

All this time, as Anna was analyzing the situation, they had been staring into each other's eyes again. He sure wasn't a flincher. His eyes were some sort of light gray-green. Hazel, she guessed you would call it. Relaxed, too. Self-confident. Suddenly, Anna felt like she was looking into a mirror. Who was this guy? Was he a pretender like she was or a highly successful day trader with digs in Pacific Heights?

She couldn't look away, but she opened her mouth to ask him if his name was really Joe. Before she could form the words, his finger came forward and placed itself perpendicular to her lips. It smelled sweet, as if he had stirred his citrus vodka martini with its tip. It crossed her mind that he had her best Elle Rosy Blush on the back of his left knuckle.

"Barry Zimmerman," he said. "You were going to ask me my real name, weren't you?"

Anna nodded slowly, transfixed by his smile. Barry held out his hand exactly as he had a quarter of an hour before. "Can we begin again?" he asked.

"Anna Weiss," she said and shook his hand.

He must have good genes, Anna thought.

But what the hell was she thinking?

Carousel Heart
By Wendy Walter

MOST NIGHTS, AFTER HER DAUGHTER surrendered to sleep, Sandra found herself alone. She would remove her shoes and loosen the cord of hair twisted at the base of her neck as she walked down the hall, past her bed, and into the bathroom.

After locking the door she left the lights off and shivered in the echoing dark, letting her breath grow ragged. When the tears came, she pressed a towel hard against her face and allowed her sorrow to loosen, then rip apart the artifice of her life. Shoulders heaving, her cries silenced by the soft, nubby surface of the towel, she reduced herself to a hard, still lump. Some nights, it took hours to spiral through the pain. When she finally came out on the other side, she refolded the towel and straightened it on the rack while waiting for her breathing to slow. With swollen eyes shut, she diligently reworked the constructs of her life. Only after her near-perfect posture returned would she turn on the light. She always avoided the mirror while she splashed her face with water. Then she would patter downstairs to find something to help her sleep. Usually it was vodka.

She thought about the jagged little circus tune starting up in her head every morning as she sipped her coffee, then slipped into the trappings of her own private circus. To the naked eye, Sandra was perfection, sailing through life, using her wide-toothed smile to navigate. She circumvented snarls of politics at fundraisers and shaped her causes into hives of efficiency. People warmed to her, then quailed after she whirled past and left them bobbing in her wake. But if anyone hesitated before accepting a dinner invitation, Sandra never noticed. At least if she did, she never let it show.

Her husband, Henry, was proud when he thought of her, and praised her when he happened to be home. He would have purchased a mansion on the Curl for her, but she had chosen instead to build a new home across the river, claiming it would have a better view. She had been right, of course. Many others followed, challenging the island's long-held social dominance by erecting edifices of southern taste and charm to stand alongside Sandra's overlooking the Curl.

The great Mississippi fashioned the Curl when it meandered back on itself and surrounded a curling sliver of land with slow, rolling water. Some water never escaped its loop, as an ever-circling ribbon of debris caught in its current confirmed. But this didn't stop the wealthy from thinking the Curl was the most exclusive community south of the Mason-Dixon line.

Sandra knew Henry loved his house and their life, but it was soon very clear that he loved his work best. Most nights found her curled in the window seat, swigging vodka out of the bottle as she traced the moonlight across the river to the Wellington estate. The mansion was artfully settled into the landscape, surrounded by thousand-year oaks. Its lush lawn draped over the folds in the hillside all the way down to the boathouse. Tonight, however, something was wrong. There was a light on in the old boathouse. It startled her. No one had gone near it for years. Not since Callen had left.

Perhaps she was tired and had downed too much vodka that night, but the boathouse light wriggled through her defenses and flooded her with memories of Callen and the moments they had shared.

I want that...

It had started simply enough, with a dare. There were five of them that night, drinking beer and rolling around the back of a van, looking for something to do. School had finally ended. Though most would try on a shiny new collegiate self the following autumn, that night they vowed to stay together forever.

But Sandra was different. Her family didn't live on the Curl, her father just worked there, managing the estates where the other kids lived. As a child she had played with the kids in the big houses while her father constructed palatial additions for their parents. He had also gentled their horses, refereed their neighborhood feuds, and helped them wrestle their demons while helping himself to forty-year-old bourbon in their smoky, paneled dens. At the end of the day, he and Sandra would take the bridge back to their tiny, rented house, where he would drink some more.

Sandra noticed the casual way the kids broke their toys and ruined their clothes. Things were easily replaced in their world. People too. New mommies, girlfriends, and uncles (who weren't really uncles) cycled around the Curl on an unending merry-go-round. Everyone raced to be first and best. Sandra did her best to fit in. She learned early how to ape the bored contempt her Curl friends acquired in their teenage years.

That night in the van, the beer made everything feel right. A carnival was just leaving town. They drove by the park and noticed a herd of carousel horses, bright and shiny in the headlights, leaning against crates, frozen mid-gallop and prance. But Sandra's eyes had been on Callen when she whispered, "I want that."

Another boy raised an eyebrow. "Dare you, Callen."

Callen grinned. The brakes grated as the van came to a halt. They clambered out, full of suppressed laughter, and heaved a horse, pole and all, into the van. Then they roared off to Callen's boathouse where they danced around the horse in wild celebration.

Sandra still remembered the feel of Callen's lips, how his soft hair took the moonlight and how the devilish turn of his grin tweaked her heart. They danced closer and closer until there was nothing between them. After the others left they moved to the big red sofa. Sandra found she almost couldn't breathe. Then she found she didn't need to. Being with him, she discovered, was life enough.

They spent as much time as possible at the boathouse that summer. Sandra was surprised to learn Callen hated his well-heeled life and plotted to escape the trappings of the Curl as soon as possible. He generously included Sandra in his dreamy rambles. Together, they mapped out the mad adventures they would have once they struck off and forged a new path. The light in his eyes seemed to match her own. By the end of summer, she trusted him with her heart and shared her secrets and simple wishes with him. He seemed to listen, but then...

Sandra shook away the memories and looked down at the vodka. Some nights it required the better part of a bottle before she felt brave enough to sleep. This night would be no exception. The stars had faded when she finally stumbled upstairs. Stretched out, alone in her oversized bed, she found peace for a few hours.

❖

The next morning dawned wintry and dreary. She donned her pearls and something Chanel. Rehearsing her smile, she drove Alexia to the private kindergarten on the Curl. She flicked on the headlights as they rounded the curve near the Wellington's gate. The beams of light grazed two men in jumpsuits maneuvering a stained red sofa into the back of a Salvation Army van. A jumble of boxes, lamps and clothing awaited a similar fate nearby.

Alexia stopped humming in the back seat and pointed. "Look Momma, a horse!"

And there it was, leaning against a stack of boxes. The tarnished pole was almost unrecognizable but the carousel horse still looked bright and fresh. Sandra felt a tick begin in her left eye as one of the men threw it into the truck.

"Momma, I want that."

Sandra smiled hard into the rearview mirror and struggled to keep the despair out of her voice as she whispered, "We'll see, sweetheart."

Alexia was not to be placated. As her daughter's demands escalated to screams, Sandra gripped the wheel with white knuckled hands and drove straight down the middle of the road to the school, trying not to think about why the Wellingtons had cleaned out the boathouse. Callen had been the only one ever to use it.

Sandra's smile was wooden as she unbuckled her daughter and watched her race out onto the playground, her tears forgotten. Two women Sandra had known all her life walked past.

"...they didn't find much," one of them was saying. "In those circumstances, they never do. Anyway, he's home, you know."

"Callen?" said the other. "They must be planning something."

"Whatever it is, the Wellingtons will do it well."

Sandra's back went ramrod straight when it hit her. It had been Callen in the boathouse the night before. Perhaps her expression *was* slightly frozen, perhaps she *was* overly careful when she slid back into her car, but no one appeared to notice as she took the Curl Road. She drove and drove and drove. Mindless of where she went, she concentrated on the mechanics of going, until the road curved toward the river, ending at the bank.

She stopped the car, put her head in her hands and let the pain wash over her.

It had ended just as simply as it had begun. His mother had found them, naked and entwined on the red sofa, making plans to hitchhike around the world before settling in a tin-roofed shack in the Caribbean. His mother had watched them dress, her eyes sliding off Sandra as if she were a frayed throw pillow. But Sandra saw only Callen's smirk as he buttoned his fly. He hadn't even said goodbye when she skittered out the door.

They shipped him off to West Point the next day. Sandra had waited to hear from him, but it was months before he returned her calls. By then, there were only awkward silences between them.

Sandra had run into his mother, whose smile had held just a twinge of nasty as she noted Sandra's knock-off Gucci sandals. "I have nothing against you, child, but there is nothing much in your favor either. Forget him, darling." Sandra smelled the money in the older woman's perfume as she leaned forward. "You weren't the only one, you know."

Until that moment, Sandra had pretended not to care when she heard about his other girlfriends. But something in the cool swish of his mother's skirt galvanized Sandra to action. She knew suddenly how well she could play that game. After all, she'd had a front row seat in all the best houses on the Curl. She could be equally unhappy, rich or poor, and rich would be far more fun. So she maxed out her credit cards at the designer outlets and buttonholed Henry at a party the very next week. They married the following year. Since then, Sandra had been perfecting her spiraling glide through the biggest and best houses on the Curl. She wasn't sure exactly when it had happened but there had come a moment when Callen's mother had not been able to keep the envy off her face as Sandra sailed by.

Callen was rarely home after that summer. Occasionally Sandra had spotted him across a room, down the block, or slouched in the back of an expensive car but so far she had managed to avoid any close contact.

The light had faded by the time Sandra came to her senses. It was humiliating to think that he, alone, had touched her heart. She had Henry and her daughter. She had friends and social successes. It was long past time to get over Callen. Her right turns, graceful pivots in doorways, and sudden headaches at parties had to stop. Did it matter if he knew her mad scuttles into the shadows were to avoid him? She couldn't, *she wouldn't*, do it anymore.

She called home and asked Esperanza to put Alexia to bed.

It was dark by the time her car rolled soundlessly down the drive. She collected the gas can, crept down to the river and out along the pier where she untied the rowboat. Silently, she rowed across the current to the boathouse.

Her hands jittered as she slopped gas on the decorative nets, antique rocking chairs and pink azaleas tucked under the low eaves. It took seven tries to strike the first match. When the flame sputtered to life, she laughed in surprise. It echoed through her, sounding tinny and odd, but for the first time in years, she felt as if she was moving forward. The bushes took first, the leaves curling as they surrendered to the flames. The smoke made her lightheaded and giddy.

It wasn't until after she trotted back to the rowboat and untied the line that she noticed the light inside the boathouse. It was just a naked bulb on a string, but combined with the flames, now licking the eaves, there was just enough light for her to see the narrow, seven-foot long brass-handled box laid out on the table. Callen had, indeed, come home.

She sank to the floor of the rowboat, limp with shock. Of its own accord, the rowboat swerved, then worked its way into the current. By the time the fire engines pulled into the Wellington's drive, the boat had drifted halfway around the Curl. Eventually, it would loop back around, as did all the flotsam and jetsam of the Curl, relentlessly tugged on by its cycling current.

The bottom of the rowboat was awash with water. It seeped into Sandra's clothes as she lay there, staring up at the stars and wondering about it all. If her life ebbed away just then, would the boat continue circling the Curl forever?

But then she noticed it, a hitch in the wheezing, pipe-organ tune that constantly played inside her head. It tickled her hollowed-out places. She waited for it to come around—there it was again, a break in the melody. Was it big enough for her to slip through? Perhaps not—though if she worked hard...

She pondered this until the river's chill drove her to slap an oar in the water. With deep strokes, she struck out against the river's flow.

Dawn was still hours away when Sandra found her way back to shore. If anyone had been about, they might not have noticed how relaxed her shoulders appeared or recognized the flawed tune she hummed. Later, she learned Callen had died from a roadside bomb while serving as an aid for a high-ranking general, one who also lived on the Curl. Callen's body was never found.

The coffin, which had burned with the boathouse, had been empty.

Back Story of the Back Road
By Eileen Malone

THE MORE SHE DROVE, THE MORE FRANTIC she became, her stomach shooting acid into her esophagus. The clients were expecting her. She had all the paperwork needed to finalize the deal. She was going to be frazzled, sweaty, and very, very late—that is, if she even made it there. Probably best to simply go back home. Come back another time with better directions.

Of course the damn off-ramp that her map said she should take was closed and the detour brought her to unfamiliar crossroads. Right or left? She tossed an imaginary coin and turned left. As she drove, she noticed street signs disappearing, no more traffic lights or stop signs, the road becoming more and more potholed, and the freeway far, far behind her. She drove and drove, getting deeper and deeper into a rural landscape. She drove past farmland and fallow fields and cattle, further and further away from civilization. She drove on the narrow two-lane highway sandwiched between a tractor and a mobile home, without even a shoulder where she could pull over and fish her cell phone out of her purse to call for help. But who the hell could she call? And where the hell would she say she was?

Always the stress, the pressure, the looming decision that was a lose-lose situation. Her husband was always leaving important things for the last minute, imploring Marcy to drop this off or run this over there or pick that up over here. And she did. She did because he really was a decent guy, faithful and loyal. And she didn't know how not to.

Zack would be furious if she came home without the papers signed. Damn him and his quick temper and disorganization. Damn his cheapness. Instead of hiring an assistant, he dumped everything he didn't want to do on

Marcy. Damn how he'd said, when he proposed, that she would never have to work, except of course, to help him. Damn how he had her take computer and real estate classes. Damn how he shared her Notary status with whomever he felt like. *Marcy'll do it. No problem.*

Damn herself for doing whatever he asked.

Every morning they reviewed yesterday's list and pulled together today's list over coffee—black—and generic cereal served with two-percent milk. Every morning, Monday through Friday, they listed groceries and household maintenance chores waiting to be completed. Every afternoon, she worked at doing what he referred to as "straightening things out" and what she referred to as keeping his books, paying his bills, correcting his mistakes, soothing his worried clients, and arguing to no avail that he could afford an assistant, and should hire one.

"Not with the kid in college," was always his response. He insisted they couldn't manage another salary. Anyway, no one else could do as good a job as she did.

"Slave labor," she responded, deadly serious behind the smile.

God, it was hot. She turned on the air conditioner before she remembered it didn't work. Somehow, taking the car in to have the air conditioning fixed never transferred itself from a yesterday list to a today list. She opened the window and hot air blew her hair into her mouth. No gas stations, no businesses, no side-of-the-road fruit stands. Nothing. She closed the driver's side window and opened the passenger side. Better.

❖

It was then she saw the fork in the road and the structure beside it. There was a sort of hut, or shed, with a few pickup trucks in front. She pulled in and parked in the shade under the sign that said "Tiny's Joint." She did a quick rearview mirror check. Ran her fingers through her hair and re-clipped its thick blackness to cover the odd streak of gray here and there, pulling it up and back. Swiped some pink gloss on her lips and cheekbones and blinked her eyes, pupils especially dark in the afternoon shade.

A warm breeze had come up and when she climbed out it blew her skirt apart where it buttoned down the front. She didn't care. Let it blow up and even wrap itself around her legs. She approached the shed and leaned into the door to push it open.

"I'm so lost!" She almost shouted it as she looked around. Tiny's Joint was small, no pool table, no juke box, just a dozen barstools and open, unshaded windows letting in daylight and fresh air. It was clean and smelled like hops.

A young man and woman seated at the far end of the bar playing liar's dice looked up at her. "No you're not," the woman said, smiling. "Not anymore."

Another man sitting on the bar stool right in front of Marcy swung around. She almost gasped aloud. He was movie-star handsome in a movie-star cowboy kind of way. Blue, blue, blue eyes. Paul Newman blue. Wavy hair curling at the nape of his neck, brown with streaks of sun-bleached gold. He smiled a Steve McQueen grin.

"Where are you going?" he asked softly, looking directly into her eyes.

"Douglas?" She replied as if it were a question.

"Well, all ya havta do is turn around and go back the other way. Somewhere along the way you jogged left when ya shoulda jogged right."

"That makes sense," she sighed. "The off-ramp was closed and the detour wasn't marked."

"Sit yourself down." He patted the bar stool next to him. "Lemme get ya a nice cold beer so you can pull yourself back into yourself."

"Oh no, I couldn't drink and drive. I've got an appointment in downtown Douglas. That road, the one I came in on, that's the one I should take back?" She dreaded another hot drive.

"Oh, it'll get you there all right, straight there. No turns, no decisions, just straight. C'mon, one beer won't hurt you. As a matter of fact, from the looks of you, I'd say it'll do you some good."

She took a deep breath. The young couple waved from across the bar. "You were lost but now you're found," the young woman said in a sing-song voice.

Why not? she thought. Why the hell not? Screw Zack and his last-minute emergencies. Screw him for not making enough money to support them without putting his wife to work. Screw the acid reflux she was dealing with, the headache she would probably have on the long drive home in Sunday afternoon traffic. Screw the car with no air conditioning.

Here she was in the middle of nowhere, being offered a beer in a quaint, cool bar by an amazingly handsome cowboy, and she was hesitating? Sometimes she believed she deserved the misery her daily life doled out to her.

"Well, thank you, yes. I will have that beer."

He held out his hand for her to shake. "Ted."

She shook it. "Marcy."

His hand was rough but gentle. The bartender turned out to be the young woman, who went behind the bar to fetch a cold beer and a chilled glass. "This one's on the house." She smiled and tapped her knuckles on the counter.

Marcy settled on the bar stool next to Ted, who poured the beer into her glass and handed it to her. She took a long swallow, then another. Never had she had a thirst so satisfied. "This is the best beer ever," she said.

"Plenty more where that came from, little lady." he clicked his bottle to her glass. "What's the big rush to get to Douglas?"

"Work." She waved her hand dismissively. "Doing a job I hate, for a boss I hate." She couldn't believe she said that. She looked to see his reaction. Once again he stared back into her eyes, seriously, deeply. She looked down at her hands cooling around the icy glass. The veins popped, purplish under her skin. She dropped her hands to her lap.

"Shame," he clucked. "What kind of work do you do?" He swigged from his bottle.

"I work for a realtor. Run his errands, get his paperwork signed, sealed, and delivered."

"Even on Sundays?"

"Oh yes, part-time on weekdays and always all day on weekends so he can be meeting and greeting possible buyers at open houses. And you? What do you do?"

"Odd jobs hereabouts. Fix farm equipment mostly, and help out with cattle. Folks in these parts keep me busy."

"Somehow it doesn't feel busy out there."

"Yup, and that's why I like it." His grin was absolutely disarming. "I've got a trailer hooked up behind a rancher's big old house. I keep an eye on the house and the dogs when he goes off traveling. I get up when I feel like it, go to bed when I feel like it, eat and drink whatever I want, and life is good."

She must have looked envious because he stopped talking and tapped her shoulder. "Hey, look at me, here with a beautiful young woman, drinking beer on a warm Sunday afternoon and wondering if she would like another."

"My goodness, I drank that down quick." Marcy lifted her glass. That comfy feeling that comes with drinking on an empty stomach was settling in her thighs quite nicely. "One more shouldn't do any damage, do you think?"

Just then the door opened and in walked two men in jeans, boots, and tee shirts. They slapped Ted on his back, winked at her, and settled themselves down as the barkeep served up shots of tequila and beer backs.

"Ted," one of the guys called out. "Ain't ya gonna introduce us to the pretty lady?"

"Marcy. I'm Marcy." She waved in their direction. "I was lost."

The door opened again and three more men walked in to greetings and slaps.

"Marcy." Ted leaned over her. "Looks like the shift's finished. This place'll be full in about ten minutes. I say we get the hell outta Dodge, before it gets dodgy—ha-ha."

She could feel his closeness, smell something like sandalwood. He took her elbow lightly. She pushed her glass away. "Right. I suppose I should head for home. I've totally missed my appointment and it's a long drive, especially over the bridge, late on a Sunday."

"Don't leave me, Marcy. Not yet." He tipped her chin up

with his forefinger. "It's still early. We've got hours of daylight and I'd like to show you around what you call rural. C'mon. Lock up your car and get on the back of my bike."

"Your bike? My God, I'm in a dress! And wearing these high-heeled strappy sandals."

Her cell phone rang out from her purse where it sat on the bar. "Oh dear. Excuse me," she said and took her purse and her phone outside.

It was her husband. He wasn't worried, just angry.

"The clients are looking for you. Where the hell are you? Don't tell me you got lost! The directions were perfectly clear. Couldn't be any easier. When are you coming home? And what's for dinner?"

Dinner. They ate every night at eight o'clock. That way, Zack said, it didn't interfere with business. Dinner eaten in front of the television watching whatever Zack wanted. He held the remote. Marcy cooked, served, and cleaned up.

She peered through the open door at Ted's mostly straight back with a slight sexy slouch. She unbuttoned the top button of her blouse, looked down at the crepe-like skin of her cleavage, buttoned back up again.

She let out a big breath and ignored Zack's question about dinner. "I'm on my way home," she said. "I'm okay. I don't know where I am, exactly, but I'm stuck in terrible traffic." She didn't say, *stick that in your pipe and smoke it.* She ended the call without waiting for Zack's response.

Then she locked the car and walked over to the beautiful silver and black Harley with a cushioned back seat she knew she would fit on perfectly. She touched the soft leather.

"Are we on?" There was Ted behind her. She could feel his breath on the nape of her neck. She turned into it.

"What about helmets?" They stood face to face, close enough to kiss.

"It's only the back roads. We'll go slow." Slow! She went moist at the implication.

"Oh, yes, let's do it!" This time, no backing down.

He instructed her: stand over here, face the back, put your left hand on my shoulder, put one foot on the bar, swing the other one over. She slung her purse across her chest, hiked up her skirt, and lifted herself to straddle the seat securely.

The air was the same temperature as blood. Oh yes, she was *on*. On. This time, she might stay beyond daylight. This time, she might enter the night. She wrapped her arms around Ted's waist, leaned her forehead against the back of his neck, and squeezed. Onward.

He gunned the motor.

❖

Stop.
Go back.
The detour? Yes.
The handsome man in the bar? Yes.
Her having a beer? No.
She's approaching the bridge, lost in the back story of the background, no idea how she even drove this far. The last thing she remembers is some old man in a dive bar giving her directions to the nearest freeway on-ramp.

She wonders if he had all his own teeth or hair or even a motorcycle. Each time, she travels a little further, lingers a little longer in a story that gets better and better. One day she won't come back.

She recaptures the feel of his breath on the back of her neck. Brakes behind the backed up traffic. Opens both windows so her skirt billows, allowing the air to cool her thighs. Smiles. Another day she got through.

It's wonderful how she copes.

Stocking-Board Education
By Darlene Frank

THE MAN'S GARAGE WAS A SMALL, dark pit crammed with rows of hosiery-making machines that looked like tall pumps and gave out steady whooshing, banging sounds. The air was heavy with the smell of oil. Bins of white, undyed nylon stockings crowded the corners; stray nylons lay here and there like torn-off sleeves. A woman my mother's age worked at a sewing machine, facing a wall. Next to a dingy, opaque window stood a smooth, flat board that looked like a narrow ironing board.

"How old is she?" the man shouted to my mother over the noise. He smelled of sweat and needed a shave. Mom had driven me to meet him in hopes he would hire me for the summer. His neighbor, a woman from our church, had told Mom he needed a worker. I'd just finished ninth grade.

"Fifteen," Mom shouted back.

He waved his hand. "It does not matter. I am behind in my work. I need help right away." His speech was thick with a German accent.

Mom looked at me, shocked perhaps by this dark, shouting German and the grim aspect of the garage. But the look on her face said we were lucky to have found this job so easily, that it was almost too good to be true.

"Seven-thirty to four o'clock. You can eat your lunch in my kitchen." He gestured toward the door at the top of the stairs that led into his house.

My summer looked dismal.

For years Mom had said to family and friends, "I can't wait until my daughter is old enough to go to work. She can quit school and get a job to help pay the bills." Old enough was sixteen, the legal working age in Pennsylvania, and I was always destined for the pants factory. "That's where I worked until I was married. She can do the same thing," Mom said.

I didn't believe she would make me leave school. My grandparents would have objected, the school guidance counselor would have stepped in, and I could not imagine what my rage might drive me to do. My parents didn't seem to recognize that the only students dropping out of high school in the 1960s were pregnant girls.

But like many Old Mennonites, Mom and Dad viewed schooling beyond the basics as unnecessary and suspicious because it led to worldly desires and behavior. Mom had finished eighth grade, Dad tenth. This was all they expected of their five children.

I'd been to the pants factory. When I was four years old, Mom took me a few times to visit the women she'd worked with. Rows of them sat at sewing machines, men's pants heaped on their laps, machines whirring, their voices yipping over the noise. I didn't mind these visits because I always came away with a bag of empty spools—tall cardboard cones, soft gray-brown, each one painted shiny yellow or black at the tip. I liked the way the cones stacked and smelled, their dry, pebbled texture and glossy tips. I played with them until they turned to mush in the sandbox after a rain. But the factory itself didn't interest me. I didn't want to work there as a teenager—sitting in a line, pedaling a machine, surrounded by endless chatter about casseroles and pregnancy. The idea repelled me.

I had my own vision for the future: After graduating from school I would work at a job I liked, perhaps in an office. I would live in an apartment in town where I could walk down the sidewalks and admire the pale mannequins in dress shops, wander into Musselman's linen store, and breathe the clean, cottony scent of the sheets stacked to the ceiling on tables and shelves. I'd save money for college someday.

But now, here we stood, in the hosiery mill. I would begin work the next morning.

❖

I worked at the far end of the garage next to the dirty window. I sat at the stocking board and examined the nylon hose spit out by the machines. For eight hours a day I stretched white, undyed nylons one by one onto the narrow board, pulling each stocking tight and inspecting it for runs and snags, flipping the board to check both sides. Those with runs I discarded. Those with snags I repaired, coaxing the thread flat with a small metal tool until no sign of imperfection remained. Speed was important and I had stacks of new stockings to finish each hour.

The German thumped around among the machines, hair askew, his beard a dark stubble. He was always in sight, and I could never slack off. He rushed back and forth, muttering to himself, carrying bundles of stockings to my board. He communicated only to shout orders. "Put them in the other bin!" "Throw those out!" I wondered where the stockings went after I finished with them and how they became the tanned nylons sold in stores, but I didn't ask. I did not want to show the slightest interest in this line of work.

I ate my bag lunch at his small kitchen table, savoring Mom's bologna sandwiches and canned peaches little more than the work. Now and then the German joined me to eat his own lunch. We sat across from each other on the brown banquettes, not saying a word. He was maybe forty years old; he had lost his wife and lived with his teenage son. But if he felt lonely or noticed that a young girl shared the intimacy of his kitchen, he didn't let on. I was hardly aware of it, either, my mind locked on the long afternoon that still remained of the day.

The woman who worked at the sewing machine smiled at me, though it was too noisy to talk. Each time I looked at the clock on the wall over her head, it seemed only another ten minutes had passed. The place felt like a cage. I hated the noise, the smell, the oily film that clung to my skin long after I'd left for the day. In our house we took full baths only once a week, on Saturday night, so the best I could do to rid myself of the residue was take a washcloth to my face and arms at the bathroom sink. Each night I could smell the mill in my hair as I went to sleep.

The work bored me beyond anything I had imagined. Stocking on, flip the board, stocking off. Stocking on, flip the board, stocking off. A slow, ticking death till the end of the day. Then relief, daylight, air. Only to come back tomorrow.

I was desperate for diversion from the stifling routine, and I found it—if only for a moment—in the man's refrigerator. On the shelf where I stored my lunch, I'd noticed a bottle of whiskey. Mennonites didn't drink, but I had seen whiskey in magazine ads. They showed glasses brimming with amber liquid, smooth and mysterious, cooled with ice cubes. I had long wanted to know what whiskey tasted like. One day I decided to sample it with my lunch.

I took the bottle out of the refrigerator and half filled the blue plastic cup from my thermos, then carefully set the bottle back in the same spot on the shelf so the German wouldn't notice it had been touched. I had learned, either from novels or the ads, that you mixed whiskey with water. I filled the cup to the top with water from the tap, carried it to the table, and sat down to have whiskey with my lunch.

I'd been raised on milk, shoofly pie, and fresh-picked garden vegetables, and it took only one sip to destroy any seductive pleasure I'd imagined of this drink. The taste of whiskey was so foreign, so unlike anything I'd ever put to my tongue, so shockingly bitter and revolting it stopped my thoughts. My mouth tasted like liniment. I hastily poured the brew down the sink, rinsed my cup, and retreated to my bologna sandwich.

When the German came into the kitchen, I could still smell the whiskey. But the grease in his nostrils must have masked the smell of all else because he didn't say a word. He set his plate down across from me no differently from any other day. We ate in silence, me still shuddering from his bottle, he perhaps waiting for day's end to get at it himself.

Thanks to the woman at the sewing machine, who'd reported the German to the Labor Department for hiring an underage teen, I was spared a return to the man's garage the following summer. But, alas, hosiery mills seemed to find me. At the end of my sophomore year in high school, my parents got wind of another such "factory," and the previous summer began to repeat.

The Dublin mill was housed in a clean, spacious building well-lit with fluorescents and run by a large, tight-lipped woman with a doll's face and her thin, bespectacled husband. She and I did the same mind-numbing task I'd done for the German. The machines were far enough from our stocking boards that we could talk over the noise, but neither she nor her husband said much to me. As long as I showed up on time and worked my way through the stacks of nylons, they had no reason to.

The job's saving grace was the Sparks family. Within weeks of my starting work, the mill was sold to a couple from North Carolina, who moved in and took over. Sparky was tall and tan; he moved like a cat among the machines—pulling, fixing, oiling, and adjusting—at ease and with pleasure. His wife, Zell, was a strong-boned, handsome woman with a generous smile. She examined stockings like I did. Both Zell and Sparky loved to talk and I liked their Southern drawls. They walked over to my stocking board to chat; they offered me sodas and a pillow for my chair. On our breaks they laughed and told stories, Sparky's voice high and mellow, Zell's husky and deep. Often they put an arm around my shoulders as they talked. A smooth haze of smoke from their cigarettes encircled our small group.

Zell kept saying she wanted Jimmy, their son, to take me out on a date. She thought it would be really nice of him to do that because I was such a sweet girl.

Jimmy was two or three years older than I and worked with his father at the machines. Tall, friendly, and cute, with freckles and sandy hair that was always a little mussed, he grinned at me from behind his thick glasses. I knew he was too cute to like me as a girlfriend, though, and wouldn't want to date a Mennonite girl. And I had a boyfriend then, though

I didn't mention him. I didn't want to disappoint Zell by saying I couldn't go out with her son.

❖

Summer ended and my bosses asked me to continue at the mill after school each day in the fall. Mom was pleased.

I told no one at school about my factory job except my best friend and my boyfriend. I was on the academic track and concentrated on my studies. You didn't need parental permission to say you were headed for college and, without knowing how I'd get there, I acted as though it would happen.

The guidance counselor had proposed visiting my parents. "I'd like to encourage them to send you to college," she said. "Let me come to your house and talk to them."

I vetoed her suggestion on the spot. An authority figure from the school in our living room, lobbying for an education my parents disapproved of and couldn't afford would have sent shockwaves through our household for months—just one more sign of my insubordination.

"Please don't," I begged. "It will only make things worse."

❖

Though Sparky and Zell could not shield me from the monotony of the work, their soothing presence carried me through the weeks. I doubt they knew how empty the hours examining stockings felt.

Diversions beckoned. Each day I eyed the bright green-and-white packs of Salem cigarettes scattered with the coffee cups and napkins on the lunch table. I wanted to try cigarettes, just like I'd wanted to try whiskey. I'd lingered over magazine ads—beautifully colored packages, men and women smoking together beside streams of cool water. I felt certain I would smoke as soon as I moved away from home. I planned to smoke Alpines because I liked the aqua-blue logo on the package.

On a day when I knew my parents would be gone and I'd be alone for at least forty-five minutes, I took two cigarettes from the table and smuggled them home in my purse. Two seemed necessary because I was likely to want another after I'd smoked the first. That afternoon I took a wooden match from the box Dad kept in the kitchen cupboard and looked for a safe place to smoke on our property. I chose a spot on the south side of the garage, where the grass was green and not likely to ignite if a spark hit the ground.

With the smooth, unlit cigarette in my mouth, I struck the match on the concrete wall of the garage. The noise and magnitude of the sudden flame made me nervous. I lit the cigarette and inhaled deeply. My first taste of whiskey may have been a shock, but it had not hinted at the assault of the cigarette. Over previous weeks I'd held fresh cigarettes to my nose to get used to the smell and imagined how it would feel to smoke them. But this gradual acclimation had not prepared me for taking smoke into my lungs. The heat of the cigarette felt like a blow. The fire was in my throat and chest, not on the ground where I'd worried it might end up. Smoke flared from my mouth and nose as I coughed—incredulous that cigarettes tasted so unlike a cool breeze, angry that I had been so deceived, disappointed that my dream of smoking leisurely by a stream with a man had been destroyed in mere seconds. I crushed the cigarette, smuggled the evidence back to the mill, and threw it in the trash.

Zell got her wish: Jimmy asked me out. I felt guilty because I had a boyfriend, but I couldn't turn Jimmy down. I was part of their family at the hosiery mill and he was taking me out as a gesture. I knew it wasn't a real date.

Over a hamburger at Red's Diner, Jimmy stirred his lemonade and talked. Nothing about his manner revealed he thought I was awkward at conversation or that we were there for his mother's sake.

Sparky and Zell applauded when we walked in the door of their house afterward, and Jimmy's two teenage sisters bounced into the entryway, fresh-faced and eager. "We're so puh-*leezed* to meet you," they gushed, coming close and cocking their heads to look at me. Their bright faces were even cuter than Jimmy's. Their yellow curls swung as they spoke. They wore short shorts and blouses in bubblegum colors, their long blonde legs prancing like horses'. I'd never seen such girls, not even at school. They moved like twin images on a movie screen, vibrant and beautiful. They were everything I was not. As the four of us stood there in what seemed like a long, slow ribbon of time, I wished I could be them and live in their house, with their parents, forever.

I must have seemed plain and shy to them, but they didn't act a bit snobbish. They made me feel as though they were genuinely delighted to meet me. I almost believed them.

When the Sparks sold the mill in the spring and moved back to North Carolina, I felt devastated. I don't remember the good-byes, just the sudden absence of this special family.

The job ended the day they left, and so did my future in hosiery mills. I vowed never to work in another factory or any place that felt so stifling or dreary. Yes, the mills had delivered a useful education, including a bittersweet end to naïve adolescence. But they also left a visceral memory. For years afterward, even long past college, whenever I walked past a dry-cleaning plant, the smell drifting out to the sidewalk reminded me of the mills, and a flutter of nausea rose in my stomach.

Alone
By Jo Carpignano

This tree remembers well
how things once were,
when saplings grew
and rippling waters
flowed between these rocks.

When hills and valleys
shouted vibrant green.

Now, the green earth is dry,
its nurturing expired.
Depleted soil rejects
all hope for growth.

Evaporated rivers left
deeply furrowed scars.
Eroded mountain tops have
crumbled into mounds of dust.

This last tall pine persists
from that far distant past.
Its roots sank deep
then final aquifer expired.
Its limbs now stark and bare.

From one shriveled branch
a shrunken cone slides down,
regretfully embraced
in dry exhausted earth.

A single seed slides out
from shelter far inside.
It lies exposed,
and has nowhere to go.

Trouble Sleeping
By Diane Jacobson

GLENDA'S MOTHER USED TO SAY she was lucky to have survived her daughter's wailing. "You darned near tortured me to death. I don't think I slept a full night for eleven solid years."

Once, when Glenda went away for a week at camp, her mother remembered how a good night's sleep felt and laid down the law. Glenda could choose to sleep or not, but she was on her own. No calling out for company. No rattling around the house. Unless she was on fire, *literally on fire*, she was to remain quiet and in bed, lights off. It was about time her mother got some shuteye. While her mother slept, Glenda lay in bed working multiplication tables and solving distance-equals-rate-times-time problems. Neither helped her sleep, but they did help her pass the time and landed her at the top of her advanced math classes.

As a grown woman living in her own apartment, Glenda still didn't sleep much, but this was no longer a problem. Each night in bed, as her thoughts wandered in the jellied quagmire on the periphery of sleep, a fragment of a question would light up her brain. The fragment would grow—neurotransmitters waking, synapses activating—until soon a spark bloomed to set her mind on fire, if only figuratively. The only thing left was to get up and answer the burning question. She'd hunker down at her computer and play. Her position as a tenured economics professor gave her access to giant data sets. Currency and security fluctuations, healthcare outcomes, weather, demographics, you name it. She tapped the keys softly—programming, analyzing, decoupling, and blending masses of numbers. Once she had tortured the data into submission, she'd climb back into bed and try to sleep again.

One night, as she bent low over her keyboard to explore a real estate database, she felt a sharp pain in her back. She managed to keep working until she sent her digital instructions into the data to work their magic. Only then did she turn her attention to the spot between her right shoulder blade and spine. She arched her back and then bent forward, pressing her chest onto her thighs. It felt good to move, but the movement did nothing to ease the pain. How could she have thrown out her back sitting in a chair?

In vain, she tried to loosen the tightness, contorting to reach that unreachable spot. She stood and pressed her back against a door jamb and twisted to massage out the tension. She filled a hot water bottle and lay on it for a while. Despite all her efforts—or perhaps because of them—the tension grew. It didn't spread across her back, but seemed to pull into itself, contracting and intensifying. She swallowed a few ibuprofens and lay flat on her bed, aching until morning.

Work was unthinkable. She couldn't sit in a chair. She had to keep moving. Up. Down. Bend. Stretch. Nothing eased the pain, but Glenda was a problem solver, the kind of person who didn't just wait and see. She approached the knot with the same determination she applied to her burning midnight questions. If one potential solution didn't work, she'd come at it from another angle. And another. And another. She'd keep working until she neatly and correctly resolved the problem.

Over the next several months, she purchased a can of tennis balls to rub on the spot, a physical therapy ball to drape her body over, and an electric heating pad. She visited massage therapists, physical therapists, and acupuncture clinics, and had her workstation assessed by an ergonomic consultant. Doctors, nurse practitioners, and chiropractors all offered ideas without success. She popped pills—over-the-counter painkillers, prescription muscle relaxants, and herbal remedies. The tenacious knot remained intact. She couldn't forget it for a moment, not even when deep in her work. It was always there, pulling at her, taunting her, exhausting her.

She could doze for only a few minutes before the persistent ache reached through the peace to pull her back to consciousness. One night, she lay in bed with tears running down her temples and pooling in her ears. She kicked her feet and pounded her fists in silent frustration. She rose and paced her apartment in ways that only worsened the pain. The ache pulsed a steady, painful beat. She spun on her heel and twisted her head sharply, then gasped and fell to her knees as new hot pain rushed up to her neck. She lay paralyzed on the floor, enjoying this change for a moment in spite of its magnitude, until the agony retreated to its home near her shoulder blade, bigger than ever. She crawled to the couch, hoisted herself to her feet, and shuffled across the room to the sliding glass door, flinching with each movement.

She stepped onto the patio and moved the short distance to its railing. Like that of every other apartment in her complex, Glenda's patio faced the bay. The building, held up by a series of beams and cement footings, cantilevered out over a steep hillside. She liked the view and spent a fair amount of time studying the towns, roads, and bridges below. She considered how each of the larger elements fit together, drilling down into the minutiae for a more refined, precise perspective. As her eyes trailed the span of the San Mateo Bridge, deserted but for a single pair of headlights, she circled her arms in another attempt to ease the pain. She felt a stab with each rotation. She reached one arm back, groping with her fingers to press the tight spot, and twisted in circles like a dog chasing its tail. But years of hunching over a keyboard had rendered her shoulders, chest, and arms inflexible and forward-curving.

She bent stiffly at the waist to prevent any movement of her neck and upper back and rested her head softly on the railing. She imagined—hoped for—a *pop* to rip apart the muscle fibers and release the tension once and for all.

"Trouble sleeping?" A soft voice came from the patio next door.

She jerked upright and turned toward the voice to see a bare-chested man sprawled on a lawn chair.

Until he started medical school, Howard would sleep for decent stretches of time. He wasn't sure if it was the late

45

nights studying or the cruel schedule of clinical rotations that had beaten the sleep out of him. It also could have been that his liquid intake, once a blend of water, milk, soda, and beer had now become mostly coffee and red wine. When he did sleep, he slept hard, dead to the world. Hard, but not long. Three or four naps a day rather than all at once overnight. Three hours snuggled in bed, another one or two on the couch in his office, and a couple stretched out on a hospital cot sufficed. He fell into deep and dreamless sleep mere moments after getting horizontal and his waking was just as quick. No cobwebs to shake off or bleary-eyed stumbling to the bathroom. No chance of falling back to sleep. He awoke raring to go.

During the workday or on call nights, he had plenty to do between naps. Rounds, exams, surgery, and paperwork. At home he had fewer obligations to fill the empty hours. He was free to do as he pleased. He'd read or watch crappy TV, but what really pleased him was running. He'd pop awake and be out on the road in the time it took to throw on some sweats, a hoodie, and his running shoes. He'd been stopped more than once by wary cops. A man running through town in the wee hours certainly aroused suspicion. He didn't mind, though. The conversations he had with the law were often interesting, and, even better, killed a few of the endless minutes before dawn.

But he wasn't a young man anymore and he couldn't run for hours. Anything beyond ninety minutes left his knees and heels hurting. Now he'd cover nine miles and then hunker down to bide his time until light.

Over the years he'd tried to sleep for longer stretches. He ran through a series of sleep aides. The Seascape Sounds clock radio was useless. Warm milk and hot showers warmed, but didn't settle him. Nyquil knocked him out, but he hated waking up groggy. He gave up, learned to live with it, and did what he could to battle the boredom.

Howard had slept his fill and was killing time on the padded lawn chair staring into the starless, moonless night sky when the slider next door opened. He rarely saw any of his neighbors and was surprised to see one at this moment.

A woman in an ankle length flannel nightgown stepped out, put her hands on the railing, and stared into the night. She raised her arms and spun them in slow backward circles, then reversed direction and spun them forward. He thought he heard her groan. He tensed, sure he'd been caught spying, when she twisted in an awkward circle with one arm scrabbling against her back. What the hell was she doing?

What the hell was *he* doing? He should have made his presence known earlier. It would look pretty creepy at this point. He should just stay put, lying still and holding his breath until she went back inside. Or he could try to sneak back into his apartment.

Howard conducted this internal debate, glad for something interesting to think about for once. The woman bent at the waist and thumped her head on the patio railing. He assumed she'd go inside soon. He knew he should keep quiet and wait. But his boredom got the better of him and he found himself asking "Trouble sleeping?"

Glenda felt no fear or shock, only a new pain in her back from her sudden movement.

"Always," she said, through a constricted chest and gritted teeth. "You?"

"Yeah, always." He straddled the lawn chair and sat up. He leaned towards her and squinted. "Are you okay?"

"I'm okay," she whispered, not wanting to use much air. Since the knot appeared, Glenda had learned to breathe shallowly to limit movement from her waist up. She shuffled her feet in a quarter turn so she could face him directly without turning her head. The only light came from somewhere deep inside his apartment. His hair, smashed flat on one side, looked blond, or maybe grey.

"You don't seem okay," he said.

They looked at each other for a few moments, until Glenda grew uncomfortable and turned back to the view. "Not much going on at this hour," she said.

The man rose, stepped to the railing, and looked toward the black bay. "Pretty quiet," he said.

Glenda tried to steal a peek at him but even a fractional twist of her head was out of the question. The pain had stabilized but remained steady, unrelenting, and bigger than ever, unlike anything she'd experienced before. She felt the prick of tears and drew a big breath through her nose. She tried but couldn't hold in the whimper that followed the expansion of her rib cage.

"You are not okay," he said. Without asking, he raised a leg like he was mounting a bicycle and straddled the railing between their balconies.

"It's nothing, just a knot in my back," she said and leaned away from him. The pain of the movement hit her and must have registered on her face.

"Let me help." Before she could do anything the man was behind her, his hands resting heavily on her shoulders. "Where?"

She feared that this could end badly, but her nagging inner voice was lost beneath the screaming pain. "Right side," she whispered.

"Here?" He touched her shoulder blade near her arm.

"No, more to the middle."

"Here?" He moved his hand.

"Lower."

"I can feel it," he said as his fingers moved down the clenched muscle. "Wow, that's one tight trapezius." He walked his fingers up and down the track of tension. Glenda sucked in a breath when he found the knot. "Relax. I'm a doctor." He laughed as he said it.

She managed a small "ha."

"No, really I am." He laughed again. "Hang tight, I think if I can break the tension the muscle might relax."

Glenda's throat constricted as he wrapped one hard arm across her chest and grabbed her opposite shoulder. His chest and hips pressed up against her. He moved his free hand until she felt something gently resting on the vortex of her pain. Probably his thumb.

"Try to relax." She felt his breath on her neck as he spoke. But even if he had waited a beat for her to relax, she couldn't have done so.

Here she was in her nightgown with a strong stranger's arm around her neck. *At least the pain will stop once he chokes the daylights out of me*, she thought. He'd probably hurl her body over the balcony to land splayed in the bushes. Her legs sticking out from the nightgown would be the first things the coyotes would devour. *I wonder how often people are murdered by neighbors?* she asked herself, while contemplating the appropriate algorithm to address just this question. She didn't get far.

The arm against her chest tightened against her collarbone. The pressure of the thumb on her back increased suddenly. She let loose a garbled cry and tried to escape the torture but could go nowhere.

"Relax. Breathe," he said, his voice strained with effort. The pressure on her back increased.

If she could have inhaled deeply enough, she would have screamed. But all she could muster was a whine. It felt as though the weight of an entire house, balanced on one single corner, rested right on the knot.

"Almost," he grunted against her neck as he squeezed her from the front, pressing her back into him and his tortuous thumb.

And then it all stopped. Disappeared. The pain and tension she'd lived with for months, tried everything to kill, was gone, leaving her body tingling and anticipating their return. It was as though she'd been listening to a jackhammer pounding for so long that when it stopped the silence was louder than the noise.

Howard felt the knot give way. He'd almost given up, but she was clearly in agony. When he felt the knot constrict further, he forgot about the woman attached to the hard mass of muscle fibers and refused to back down from the challenge. He pressed, deeper and harder, until it collapsed under his thumb. The woman in his arms also collapsed.

Leaning against him, she tipped her head back, shivering. Her chest rose and fell and he heard her draw deep breaths. Her shivers gave way to shakes of laughter. He held her and couldn't help but laugh too. She turned around, still pressed against him. In the dim bluish light emanating from her apartment, he could see her cheeks were damp.

"Come inside," she said. She sighed and grinned. "Come to bed."

Her fingers laced into his and she led him inside, past a computer screen actively scrolling characters, down a carpeted hallway and into a dark bedroom. She climbed onto the bed without dropping his hand and pulled him in with her, settling on her side and wrapping his arm around her as it had been on the patio. He snuggled against her and pulled a thick comforter over them.

"I'm Howard," he said, feeling sleep pulling at him.

"Hi, Howard. I'm Glenda," she said through a yawn.

"Sweet dreams, Glenda," he replied and fell asleep.

She felt herself following. No trouble at all.

When Black Robe Come
By Bardi Rosman Koodrin

I AM NET-TAH. I have breathe air for ninety-two night of clan gathers. Each winter we sit on benches in big room, not on ground under stars like in the beginning, but I still tell yesterday stories to remind men and women and to teach our children right.

I stand. "You know me. I am holder of ice clan stories. When I was young girl, my grandmother told me how our clan hunt seal and sleep in ice."

A boy stand to ask, "How cold?"

I laugh. My eyes roll up like cedar shavings when I say, "So cold you don't want to know!"

I put my arms out big and touch my fingers. "We and land are no different. We are all the same like a big circle that never ends. Seal people let us eat their flesh and be warm in their furs so seal ways rub off on us, to move fast, see far." I put my hand to eyes to show them.

I say, "My grandmother be long dead but she still come for me when my eyes shut tight in sleep blackness. She show me our clan living on other side of sky. She take my hand and we walk cross ice till we reach the moon.

"I am holder of all stories, not just Inuit. Moon people make sure I know their stories. They took Grandmother on her final walk and lifted her up in the sky."

My granddaughter know what I mean. I tell her special stories since she be small. Now her belly is swelled with child.

I tell them, "I feel Grandmother like she be alive. Other dead clan step out from living in my blood to help me tell stories too. About times when they was hungry and babies died. Nobody could break holes in ice fast enough to bury them."

All around the room I see women cry for babies lost long ago. Men rub their eyes.

I say, "I hold stories in my heart stitched tight, like my oilskin pouch. Stories keep us all alive even when our bodies die and get put in ground. You know these stories. I tell them at each clan gather because we need to remember old ways till the sun fall out of sky forever and no one is left here."

Women nod and men grunt so I know they listen.

"At every clan gather I stand and tell you what I seen and heard."

I don't tell church people. They show us paper, say year is 1904, but ice clan learn time from sun and moon. We don't talk about that, or how whales show us how to hunt them. We keep quiet when caribou wake us up and tell us to come for them.

Church people say we are in Alaska but we say no, Inuit land. When I was a girl, Grandmother told me not to touch white people so I would not turn pale like them. I know better.

I tell my clan, "The first Russians show up in wood boats. They no wait for winter ice to walk across sea like our clan did in the beginning. First came men who kill fur animals, then men in long black dresses with bright Xs hung round their necks. They talked God like we didn't have no notion of our Creator.

"Grandmother sister was beautiful as the north light shining from sky and dancing on far line of ice that go forever. Washini had red flow and was woman, but not so old she know better when a black robe wanted her."

Women cluck tongues when I say, "He be priest for Russia leader who name sound like the cigar he smoked. Black Robe gave Washini a white lady dress the day he marry her. She should have wear her fancy seal coat she sew with ivory beads carved from walrus but new husband say wear dress instead. She do it. She love him. Black Robe take her to his land far away."

All the clan go quiet when I say, "Many Inuit men went away too, after sickness come. Our clan shrivel like the corn church people plant after so many dying from pox on face, but this was brain sickness. Fever for rush of gold all way down to California. Grandmother shake her fist to stop them acting like crows squawking over shiny rocks but still they go. My husband go even when she tell him Washini passed from sight like snow in strong sun."

My mouth get dry but I go on. "When Grandmother still alive she fear moon not shine in Russia like it do here. She ask, can moon people find Washini when it be her time? Would they take Washini on her final walk and lift her up in sky?"

The clan wait for me to talk.

I shout, "I know they did because moon people take me on other side to meet Washini! She tell me not to mourn dead clan, we are all like big circle never end. Grandmother there too. She say she wrong to hold hate and fear in her heart about black robe taking Washini. So I promise both of them to hold *all* stories in my heart, even ones that hurt.

"Our clan need to know the right way *and* the wrong way to live."

I smile. "Last night Grandmother and Washini come during my sleep blackness. They say I will die soon."

The clan begin to wail. They beat their breast.

"Stop." I put up my hand. "I be ready to wear Washini's seal coat when I take my final walk cross ice and moon people come to lift me up in sky."

I point to my granddaughter. "She know all ice and moon stories, happy and sad. When I die, she will stand and talk at clan gathers. Grandmother and Washini already take her across ice in her sleep blackness. They will tell her what everybody need to remember till sun fall out of sky forever and no one is left here.

"She is Net-tah. Hear her."

The Neighbor: After the War
By Maurine Killough

it was after the war
that she reassembled things
sour tomatoes at the end of their brittle vine

it was after the carnage
and the raking of flesh
that she found herself alone
released like a nubile youth
except she wasn't

the starting over wasn't so bad
since everything she left
reminded her of him
sour tomatoes tasting of earth
pilgrimage of landlord interviews
dry roads of groaning neighborhoods
families splashing their lives in her face
until the last road to the tiny cottage
where she put everything in its place

her floors were clean
where her heart was mauled
her condiments organized
where her brain was scrambled
her windows sparkled
where her eyes were marred
and she grew a new garden
buried the war every day with her spade
worked until her back ached
and the garden was clean of the enemy

this patch was all she had left
to put her fingers into
all she had that she could keep from dying

all she had to combat the memory bombs
grow sweet tomatoes
to pick
before they would turn brown
and spit sour mash
to reap
before they would lose the war

Shattered
By Eve Visconti

IT'S THURSDAY MORNING and Florence is puttering around her bedroom. Suddenly the floor comes at her. She hears a thud and her body feels heavy. She's not sure exactly why she's on the floor or how she got there, except that her navy blue comforter is sticking out as if it had been waiting to trip her.

She lies on the soft carpet for a moment, hoping it's just a sprained knee, then slowly stands on her good leg. She twists around and starts to shift her weight onto the injured one. *Thud.* Back down she goes, landing on her behind on a power strip complete with charger cords, grazing the back of her head on the edge of her electronic keyboard.

Getting up isn't going to work. Florence lies on the floor, trying to compose herself. She must get onto the bed and to the phone on the nightstand. Mustering all her strength, she pulls into a sitting position and drags herself parallel to the bed. She rolls forward and pushes her body onto the bed with her good leg and her arms.

Her heart is pounding and she is trembling. Shock. It is surreal not to be able to put any weight on her leg.

Keep calm, she says to herself. *Bert will be home in a few minutes, and I have a phone available.*

"I've hurt my knee," she tells the woman who answers the phone at the doctor's office.

"We can give you an appointment at 2:50 this afternoon."

Florence hangs up and waits for her husband.

Fifteen minutes later, the door opens and slams shut. Bert calls out, "Hi."

"Hi. Come upstairs, I want to talk to you about something."

"We'll get through this," Bert assures her. "We'll develop systems and it'll get easier. We'll get you out of the house too. Remember—it was just a freak accident. And it's only temporary."

Somehow this fact fails to calm Florence. Suddenly she knows what it's like to be physically disabled. *I can't just walk downstairs, get in the car, and drive myself to the hospital. I feel helpless. I am helpless.*

After X-rays, a CT scan, and a consultation with Dr. Shaw in Orthopedics, the verdict is in: it's a broken leg—there on the X-ray, right below the knee. In medical terms, it's called the *tibial plateau.* The knee would have been far worse. Or the leg could have shattered. It was a clean break and there'll be no surgery. Doctor Shaw supplies crutches, orders a wheelchair, and sends her home.

Florence is about to embark on a whole new way of coping with the most minor details of life, like getting from point A to point B, going to the bathroom, getting her clothes on and off, keeping clean, and getting fed.

One of the biggest hurdles is the stairs. *Why the hell did she and her husband buy a condo with stairs?* Up the stairs, step by step on her behind. Seven accomplished, then the landing—more dragging, seven to go. And so to bed. She lies there, exhausted, in shock, in limbo.

Somehow, despite the huge physical challenges of taking care of life's necessities, Florence worries about what she'll do with her time. Her son calls. "Mom, I'm so sorry. But it's just a broken leg. You'll heal, and you'll be fine. Use the time to do something productive—like writing your novel. Think of it as a sabbatical."

Day two. Florence is settling in. She's scared, still in shock, exhausted, yet unable to sleep because of the excruciating pain. Wary of taking any medication, she decides to tough it out with Tylenol, which helps somewhat, but every time she moves the leg, even just a little, she can't help but scream.

Day three. The wheelchair arrives. She begins to learn how to move around and pull herself in and out of it to go to the bathroom and back to bed.

Day four. The monotony begins. Bed, bathroom, bed, bathroom. Exhaustion, sadness, anger, isolation, panic attacks. She's too tired to concentrate yet unable to sleep. Not hungry, always thirsty, but not wanting to have to go to the bathroom. Yet she must drink fluids; she mustn't let herself get dehydrated. She has to move her ankle and flex her muscles or she'll be weak. Worse yet, she might get a blood clot. *What about all those massive bruises?*

"Bruising is totally normal," the advice nurse reassures her.

Every day she gets a little more adept at "running" between the bedroom and the bathroom. Her emotions cycle through panic, boredom, and anxiety. Florence tries desperately to keep it together, tries not to inconvenience her long-suffering husband, who has been thrust into the role of caregiver. The role is especially hard for him because of his work. Even though he has a home office, he's in and out all day. Still, he provides all her meals and has taken on the household chores. *So sweet of him to do all this for me,* Florence thinks. *But I'm so tired of those PB&J sandwiches. Still, I mustn't impose on him too much. I've got to do stuff for myself.*

She's reminded of the classic Hitchcock movie *Rear Window*, in which James Stewart is stuck in his apartment with a broken leg, looking out at the world.

Week one. The stairs present a challenge, but seeing the downstairs after a week is a joy. The sun streams through the patio door. The place is surprisingly tidy. She never imagined that being out in the sunshine and breathing fresh air would be so gratifying an experience.

Margaret, a family friend, drives Florence for X-rays and an appointment with Dr. Shaw, who reiterates that it is "just a broken leg. You'll be back on your feet in six weeks and you've already finished one." *Less than three months to normalcy.* Another orthopedist had said six months. *Three will do just fine, thanks very much.*

Florence returns home to wait for next week's appointment to confirm that the bone hasn't moved and she won't need surgery.

Week two. More X-rays and a follow-up with Dr. Shaw. Things are on schedule.

Though the leg pain is now largely gone, Florence has developed intense back pain, mostly at night, leaving her unable to move anything but her forearms without going into severe spasms. *Why?* Since the house is not user-friendly for the wheelchair bound, twisting and turning to do simple things like hand washing has caused muscle damage. She's told this is common and advised to use ice and heat, to elevate her legs, and above all, to maintain good posture. *How can you when you ache and your muscles spasm?* And getting up to use the bathroom in the middle of the night disrupts her sleep for hours.

Florence has a condition that causes an abnormally low number of blood platelets. Dr. Huang, the hematologist who monitors her platelet count, won't let her take any aspirin-based anti-inflammatory pills that might act as blood thinners, so she's been taking Tylenol—which hasn't helped at all. Usually this anomaly has no effect on her life. However, after two weeks of back-muscle-spasm hell, Florence finally calls Dr. Shaw.

"Doctor, I'm at my wits' end. Isn't there *something* I can take? I've been in remission for nearly a year. Why can't I take any anti-inflammatories that would give me so much relief? Can't you convince Dr. Huang that it's okay?"

Thankfully, he agrees and gets consent from Dr. Huang to prescribe a non-aspirin-based anti-inflammatory drug. *Hallelujah!* The meloxicam isn't perfect but works well enough. Anything is better than what she's endured. Going to bed has become bearable again.

Countdown to freedom, day by day, week by week.

Week six. Things are progressing nicely and Dr. Shaw says Florence should start to put "toe weight" (the weight of the leg itself, not full body weight) on the leg. *How am I supposed to do that?* He shows her how, but she's still confused and is afraid of doing more damage by putting too much pressure on her leg.

"When will I be able to walk normally, Doctor?"

"Nine weeks."

Why not the eight she'd been told? She doesn't ask; she just has to accept the fact that it will take one week longer than she expected.

She has an appointment with a physical therapist, Nicole, who admits that the "toe weight" thing is tricky. Next come the exercises to increase the strength and flexibility of the knee that hasn't been bent for weeks. Experimenting with both a walker and crutches is challenging and leaves her feeling shaky and exhausted.

The brace comes off and Florence goes off the pain medication. She and Bert begin to have little arguments. Ah yes, life is beginning to return to normal. There are good days and not-so-good days. Her energy waxes and wanes, along with her spirits.

Florence and Bert are now in a rhythm of going out every two or three days, giving her something to look forward to—a meal out, a movie, her choral rehearsals, and the medical appointments that foretell her eventual return to the land of the living.

Week nine. Dr. Shaw declares the leg healed and asks her to stand and put full weight on it, hands free. It feels pretty good.

"Now, take a step."

"Ouch!" *Why does it hurt so much?* Dr. Shaw explains that there's a lot going on. The injury has damaged a whole bunch of muscles, tendons, ligaments, and soft tissue. The leg has stiffened and is weak due to nine weeks of non-use. And there's scar tissue to contend with.

Nicole prescribes more exercises in preparation for walking normally again. *This is taking so long!* Somehow Florence had thought that, after nine weeks, she'd get up from the wheelchair and walk out of the doctor's office into freedom. *Not so fast. It's going to take perseverance and patience. Healing takes a lot of energy. No wonder I'm tired all the time.*

Ironically, Florence misses the wheelchair. She had learned to zip around freely, using her hands for activities like folding laundry and carrying things. She had become useful while staying safe.

Walking again is a whole new ballgame: balancing, worrying about balancing, and overcompensating with her arms to avoid the pain of bearing down on her leg. She tells herself sternly, *You have to do it. You have no choice.*

Another two weeks go by. Slowly. She's comfortable with the walker. People tell her she is walking better. Sometimes she forgets and almost stands up to walk without thinking. Then she remembers: *you must use the walker or you might fall—again*. Still, her stamina is low and she gets frustrated.

More physical therapy, more exercises. Baby steps, then bigger steps, like learning to use stairs and getting behind the wheel of the car for the first time since her injury. *Hooray!* She graduates to a cane. The next step is—does she dare to dream?—walking on her own.

It's exhilarating but scary. What if she gets cocky, does too much, and falls? Her mood vacillates between hope and frustration. She begins to imagine pushing a fast-forward button toward the time when she is, once again, whole.

How will she look back on this experience once life is back to normal? What wisdom will her weeks of recovery have brought? Florence takes stock.

Her body is indeed her most precious commodity and she will need to devote more time, not less, to caring for it as she ages. This is a wakeup call to keep that body strong and flexible, to maintain her balance, and to pay attention at all times.

Walking is a privilege and a joy. She should not take for granted the ability to move without effort, to propel herself from one place to another without assistance, to be a fully functioning physical being. Life's little chores aren't a nuisance. They're evidence that she is healthy and independent.

She has been surprised by the kindness of strangers and mere acquaintances, and disappointed by those she thought were closest to her. It takes a village, and villages are nearly extinct these days. E-mails are nice, Facebook is fun, but they don't get you fed or take care of your angst.

This experience has made Florence more resilient, more mindful, and more empathetic. She's taken time for reflection, read several books, seen lots of films, listened to music, and learned to cherish the life that will soon return. Never again will she doubt her ability to adapt to and learn from an experience that can shatter life—forever—in a matter of seconds.

Now, when Florence sees others in wheelchairs or using walkers, she recalls the unspoken bond she had with them while she was temporarily in their shoes, a kind of camaraderie. She knows all too well how challenging their lives are and how brave many of them are. She understands why they have fought so hard for accessibility. She has become a fervent advocate for making *everywhere* accessible to *everyone*.

Five months. Florence is well on the road to recovery. She's using the cane less and less, more for confidence than anything else. *So close, so very close.*

Some say six months is the Holy Grail of complete recovery. Others say a year. *Which is it?* It's driving her slightly crazy.

Everyone's different, and recovery isn't a black-and-white thing. One day it seems as though the break never happened. Her leg feels strong and flexible, and she hardly notices it, but then, suddenly, the stiffness, pain, and fatigue return.

There's a scar on Florence's tibia where the break occurred, but her shattered psyche will take even longer to heal than her leg.

From the second floor, Florence looks down at the seven steps to the landing. She hesitates, remembering her instructions from Nicole, "Up with the good, down with the bad," and puts her bad leg on the first step. Should she put her good leg on the same step or go down one more—like normal people do? *What if I trip and fall?* She puts her good leg on the same step as the bad one. She's not ready for regular—reciprocal—stair climbing yet.

She thinks of what it was like to pull herself up and down the stairs on her butt. *Just look how far I've come!* A wave of joy and confidence washes over her.

She flashes back to the day when nothing eventful was supposed to have happened. *Thud.*

It was *just a freak accident, wasn't it? I* will *recover fully, won't I? It won't ever happen again, will it?*

Florence puts her bad leg on the next step and continues down the stairs.

Fowl Consequences
By Laurel Anne Hill

I DROVE MY CHEVY PICKUP around a curve in Tilden Park. The middle-of-the-night fog hung thick as paste. Gina glared in my direction from the passenger's seat. I managed a glance in return. Her scrunched black-bead eyes fired virtual death rays at my baby blues. She was pissed. All because I'd pawed her a little at tonight's bash. Hey, she'd started it.

First she'd invited me for a private dip in our host's hot tub. Next she'd removed the top of her bikini in the spa. I'm talking about the same gal who believed dancing was only for married couples. What crazy part of the world did Gina call home? At least she didn't know I'd snapped a revealing shot of her amazing body when she'd closed her eyes and taken a slow, deep breath. If I couldn't touch, I damn well wanted to remember the looking part for a long time.

A car approached from the opposite direction on the two-lane road, the first vehicle I'd seen since entering the park. The idiot drove with his brights full-blast. In this soup? Like, get real.

Ricocheting beams forced my eyeballs to veer right. Bling on Gina's filmy black fantasy dress sparkled, her shoulders bare except for narrow straps. Metallic green streaks in her brown hair glistened like exotic feathers. Even her long chiffon sleeves, joined to her dress at the level of her low-cut neckline, rippled with sensual waves. The temperature inside this old Chevy bucket of bolts turned toasty. Time to concentrate on the road.

The vehicle passed. Did I see a feather-studded jacket on the dude behind the wheel? Wow. A full moon, even when hidden, could sure bring out the weirdos. My hands gripped the steering wheel. Still no word out of Gina. Nothing any full moon could do about that.

Right before the midnight hot tub disaster, Gina and I had held hands and watched funky horror DVDs with her friends. Last weekend, we'd rented a pedal boat at the local lake. I hadn't had such a good time going out with a woman since I turned thirty. Five way-too-long years ago.

Now I wanted to take that fun Gina out again. I needed to break the silence.

"I told you," I said, "I'm sorry."

"Except you're not all that sorry, Harry." She pouted her full red lips. "You don't seem to understand. Looking at me is a free gift but touching like you did without permission has—consequences. And you took that picture without my consent, too."

Damn, I hadn't realized she'd seen me do the photo. Now what was I going to say?

"Delete the picture." I tossed her my cell phone. "I never intended to post it anywhere but on my imagination."

"So crows the rooster." She shrugged. "I thought you had real regard for my feelings. I thought you were different from all those other men I've met. I liked you enough to trust you some. To show you part of the real me. And you let me down."

Whoa, I had messed up big time. My brain shipped warmth to my face. How could I turn "liked" back into "like?"

"I promise," I said, "not to act so clueless again."

"There's no return," she said, "once you step off the path of acceptable behavior. Besides, if you were a woman, wouldn't you want men to treat you with respect?"

"Please." I leaned back in my seat. My leather jacket squeaked. "Give me another chance."

Gina let out a lengthy sigh. She sounded more frustrated than forgiving. My stomach knotted and my shoulders sagged. Some soft music might help ease the tension. I switched on my iPod.

"Incredible" by the Shapeshifters led the song shuffle. How did that lively piece end up on this particular playlist? Oh, well, the song wouldn't last long. Nor would the rest of this date. In less than a half hour, I'd drop Gina off in Lafayette and head home to Berkeley. Would she relent and let me see her again? At least I'd e-mailed myself that photo of her. Oh, my God! Gina had my phone. If she found that e-mail, any chance to mend our relationship would turn deader than dead.

I rounded another curve. Damn, it was hard to see the road in this murky haze. Something huge darted across my path. A flurry of brown and red shimmered in my low beams. What the shit?

I swerved. Gina screamed. My foot slammed the brake. The truck skidded, spun around, then came to a spine-jarring halt. What the hell had I nearly hit? Or had it tried to hit me?

Gina leaned against the side window. Her hands cradled her cheeks and chin. At least the airbags hadn't deployed and complicated matters.

"You okay, Gina?" Her skin never had much color. Hard to tell if she'd gone into shock.

"Don't know yet," she said. "My head's still all weird."

Gina's head was always weird. Came from being a twenty-five-year-old virgin. An unhealthy state of non-affairs.

"I'm dizzy," she added, "and my stomach's horrid. Will you help me climb down?"

Gina hadn't drunk much wine at the party. If she ended up barfing, though, better to have her use the side of the road. I parked, then turned off the engine, leaving the lights on.

I opened the door and slid out of the Chevy. My shin banged against metal. A good thing I wore jeans. As my Nikes met hard, dry ground, my ankle turned. How had I managed to do that? My groan blended with a gobbling sound. Wild turkeys. Those winged invaders were everywhere in the East Bay these days, like they planned to take over the world. Except wild turkeys probably limited their planning to eating and mating. Some horny tom may even have dashed across the road a few minutes ago to meet up with his hot date.

The headlights dimmed. My sick car battery turned sicker. I grabbed a halogen spot light from behind the seat, then reached in and turned off the truck's lights.

"Are you all right with the dark?" I said to Gina, who remained slumped against the passenger door.

"I guess so," she replied. "Harry—"

"Yes?"

"Do you ever wish—" She burped and hand-cranked the window down a couple inches. "—that you could change what you are? Or stop the inevitable?"

"Yeah," I replied. Where was this line of conversation going?

"Me too," she said, her voice soft.

The turkey sounds came from multiple directions. The guys gobbling. The gals yelping and cackling. Wait a minute. I used to watch the nature channel. These birds weren't night prowlers. They ought to be asleep in the trees. I pushed the light's on-button and checked out the fog-cloaked surroundings. Pines. Eucalyptus. Other trees and bushes of some sort or another. Not a turkey in sight. The gobbling grew louder. Super creepy.

I limped around the front of my vehicle and navigated to the passenger's side door. I heard a soft thunk. Gina had pushed down the locks on her side and mine.

"Hey," I said. "Open up."

"I wish I could."

She clutched my cell phone in one hand and her switched-on keychain flashlight in the other. I grasped the door handle and shined the halogen lamp into the truck. Her dark eyes sparkled. The rest of her expression didn't. A bad feeling iced my already chilly bones.

"Gina, babe," I said, trying to sound calm. "What gives?"

"Did you enjoy the second movie we saw this evening?" Gina set down her mini-flashlight, then twisted strands of her emerald-streaked hair around her index finger. The gobbling intensified. "The one about the side-show freaks?"

Those deformed dudes who'd turned a trapeze artist into a duck woman? A classic horror movie—grittier than the shape-shifting hawk thing we'd seen before dinner. But why talk now about people turning into birds? The volume control for the nearby gobbling dialed even higher.

"Come on," I said, "let me in. It's late." Damn, I could hear my irritation and uncertainty rising as fast as the background turkey chatter. "Tell me your problem."

"That photo of me was in your sent mail." She waved my phone at me. "You e-mailed it to yourself."

"Because you're beautiful." What else could I say? "That's why I did it."

"A real man asks for consent. It's part of the ritual." Gina gestured with one palm facing up and fingers spread. "Even those tom turkeys out there in the trees know enough to do a special dance and get consent."

She plopped my phone down on the empty driver's seat. So close and so out of reach. Like the keys and remote to my Chevy. Consent and consequences. I twitched. Car brakes squealed from somewhere. A small voice inside my brain screamed, "Watch out."

I worked my way back to the driver's side of my truck. A door slammed not far away. In the thickening mist, my spot light caught an approaching mass of brown. . . feathers. Huh? This must be the screwball we'd encountered earlier on the road. Big dark pupils stared in my direction. The guy stopped several feet away from me. This bastard had me backed against the side of the truck.

Now his gray throat turned red, blue, and white. A tan-yellow beak opened wide. Holy crap! I didn't face some crackpot in a feathered costume. I faced a real turkey—frigging tall as me—wearing battle colors. This monster must have weighed two hundred pounds.

"Go away," I hollered.

The spurs on the turkey's legs shone through the mist like sharpened daggers. I stretched out my arms to the sides to look bigger. My ankle wobbled. No way could I run fast, even if I wanted. And this creature might be strong enough to smash a window and hurt Gina. She may have locked me out but a real man wouldn't leave her to fend for herself.

The turkey spread two huge wings. One swipe of those feathered appendages would knock me to the ground. And then what? The creature looked at me like a zombie eyeing a bucket of brains, the ugly crimson floppy things on its neck and beak the color of blood. Turkeys were birdseed and mosquito munchers—weren't they?

"Gina, honk the horn," I said.

She just sat there doing nothing. What was wrong with that woman?

The bird bobbed its head forward. I shielded my face with two arms and the lamp. The beak stabbed the back of my hand. Blood gushed from the wound. Oh, my God. The thing had opened my vein.

"Call 9-1-1," I shouted.

I ducked and lunged to the left. My ankle gave way. I stumbled, tumbled, and wound up lying on my side, facing my Chevy and looking my own spot light in the eye. The ground felt sticky. That was my blood watering the greenery. I pressed my palm against my hemorrhaging hand.

"What do you expect? Otto's always had a crush on me." Gina climbed over to the driver's seat, rolled down the window, then giggled. "Now slip that bloodied hand into your jacket pocket. Do you want every turkey in the neighborhood pecking at your wound?"

A turkey named Otto for a boyfriend? Oh, sure. Gina frigging made fun of me—of the fact that some crazed fowl wanted me for an early bird special. Had she arranged all this as a gag or for revenge? But where could anyone order up a six-foot-tall turkey?

"Smile," Gina said.

I rolled onto my back. Gina leaned out the window and raised my phone. She held her pink keychain flashlight in her other hand and took a picture. The Big Bird from Hell had attacked me and all she could do was snap a shot. Gina let out a melodic laugh. The turkey, with the grim face of an executioner, towered over me and didn't flinch.

"Gina," I pleaded, "for Godsakes."

"I'll always want to remember what you looked like before—" She smoothed the sleeves of her black dress. "Oh, Harry. I'm truly sorry Otto bit you. I'm sorry things turned out this way. I wanted you for myself." She pressed her lips together. "I guess the least I can do is show you the rest of the real me."

"Shit," I yelled. Fuck the sorry and real-me bit. Otto kicked dirt in my face. I blinked several times. "Call off Otto and let me in."

But Gina was no longer there. Instead, a turkey—less than twenty pounds—climbed out the window and flew to the top of the truck. Only this fowl—mostly plain as a hen—had head feathers the color of dark rum, slender, delicate feathers tinged with exotic streaks of green.

Gina? But that was impossible. Yet if this bird wasn't Gina, where had she gone?

A song blared from the cab of my truck. "Incredible" again. My head pounded with every heartbeat. My mouth turned dry. When I'd gotten out of the truck, Gina had asked me about stopping the inevitable. Now two pairs of beady eyes held me helpless in their crosshairs. Thick mist swirled around me like rope. What was the inevitable?

My skin itched and stung. Sharp pains stabbed my head. More blasted my chest. Gina and her buddy weren't touching me in any way I could tell. My body parts hurt like crazy all by themselves.

I had to try to get out of here. I rolled onto my side. My arms wouldn't work right. I couldn't push myself up off the ground. The lamplight illuminated the back of my wounded hand. Junk coated it and wouldn't shake free. What the hell was happening?

I moved my hand closer to the lamp. My skin was brown and tan. And fluffy. Fluffy! Fucking crap. Feathers sprouted from my hide the way werewolves in movies sprouted hair. That bite!

"Consequences," the memory of Gina's voice shouted.

A flock of tom turkeys moved out of the fog in my direction. The face and throat of their leader—the boyfriend with an attitude—blushed crimson and blue. His tail fanned. Wings down, he strutted and gobbled. This looked like some sort of a warped mating dance. Did he plan to fight me for Gina's favors? Triple fucking crap. I was screwed.

Then I saw them, another set of approaching headlights on the road. I was saved. I opened my mouth to shout for help. Instead, I yelped and cackled. My voice! What happened to my voice? My mouth made the sounds of a fucking hen turkey.

I tried to scream. My she-cackles joined the surrounding gobbles and echoed through the night.

A Hopeless American Parent
By Emily Eddins

I AM EXPERIENCING a parenting identity crisis. The reason? I am an American.

If you have been in a bookstore lately, you may have learned that American parents are the worst kind. Two popular parenting books currently on shelves inform me that to parent successfully I must emulate either the Chinese or the French. I must either become a Tiger Mom or I must teach my two-year-old that he is expected to eat Camembert while sitting quietly at the table for three hours with the adults.

The implication is that the American way of parenting needs fixing. But telling me to be a Chinese or a French parent is like telling me to *be* Chinese or French. I am an American, for better and for worse. We all know the French are culturally superior; that's nothing new. If our *foie gras* and fashion are inferior to theirs, it should come as no surprise that our children are, too. And the Chinese—well, they are the Chinese, for God's sake. No matter how many alphabet blocks I stack or flash cards I flash, my kids may never catch up.

Let's reconsider the guilt we feel for the original sin of being American parents. Wouldn't it be liberating to discover that the volumes of divergent parenting advice we unsuspecting mothers are barraged with is a load of hogwash? We would have license to ignore it in favor of parenting with good, old-fashioned common sense.

One thing I know from raising my sons is that *good* parents, no matter what country they are from, raise their children based more on instinct than on what they read. I have a stack of parenting books about twenty deep and I haven't gotten past the first chapter in any of them. What's more, I couldn't tell you what those chapters were about—

because I am too busy actually parenting to retain what I read!

I have news for you if you think you have the prescription for what it takes to parent "the right way."

There is no such thing.

Each child is unique, and parents must learn the "correct" method for raising that child the hard way: through trial and error. An approach that allows one child to flourish can make another child wither. I'm not saying you shouldn't try to do your job as a parent better every day. You owe those little buggers the very best you've got. But after that? What becomes of our children is up to them. Nature has as much muscle as nurture.

But let's assume, for a moment, that there is some national or regional formula for parenting. I was born in the (not so) great state of Alabama, where the parenting doctrine of the 1970s was benign neglect. My parents let us slide around in the back seats of speeding vehicles without car seats. My mom swilled what she termed the "occasional" martini and smoked the "occasional" cigarette while she was pregnant with me. Did I mention that my brother and I were allowed to make our own bonfires in the backyard, melt ice cubes with red-hot fire pokers, and ride our bikes in and out of six lanes of traffic at the ripe old age of nine? And guess what? *I turned out okay!*

As a child, my husband—born and raised in Mississippi, which is even worse than being from Alabama—was left sweating in his father's custom van while his dad perused gun shows and pawnshops. (That's what I call a summer enrichment program for gifted youngsters.) The effect: my husband graduated from an Ivy League college and became a successful businessman. Maybe being a lackadaisical American parent actually has its benefits. I guess now I don't have to throw my baby out with his American bath water.

Which approach is right? *Laissez faire* or *laissez* nothing to chance? Do you want a creative, independent child, or do you want a robot? Do you actually think you have any control?

The bad news is that you don't have much control. The good news is that you don't have to read the hundredth parenting book you just bought. Go ahead and put it on the dusty pile with the others. Mix yourself a martini. Light a cigarette (outside of course, not while your kids are watching, and have only one).

There. Now, exhale.

A Day in the Life
of Heddi Kent, the Librarian
By Martha Clark Scala

In Johnny Crow's Garden I met Lady Chatterley's Lover
and My Cousin Rachel.
We did The Dance of Anger to Make Way for Ducklings
and Little Women.
Doctor Dolittle dropped by, sporting The Color Purple
and Holes in his brown argyle socks.
Come read The Big Book under The Red Tent with me, he said,
and then I will tell you A Tale of Two Cities.
No thanks, I replied. These are the Last Days of Dogtown.
We may only have Three Junes left.
I am writing my Memoirs of an Ex-Prom Queen; Gregor the Overlander
is my editor. He drove across A Thousand Acres with Pippi Longstocking
to this City of Flowers and The Godfather is weeding My Secret Garden.

So, quash your Great Expectations.
If you don't, I will summon The Exorcist because
it is a sin To Kill a Mockingbird
while humming the Song of Solomon.

June Daze
By Sue Barizon

I REMEMBER GOING HOME alone from school when I was a kid. My family lived a breezy four blocks from Beresford Elementary in San Mateo, California. My younger brother, Mark, older sister, Angie, and I managed to elude each other immediately after school—much as we did at home. We grew up in the 1960s, treading the stormy waters of our parents' marriage. Mom's mental illness joined in unholy union with Papa's old-world Italian ideals. We fended for ourselves, each honing his or her own system for navigating through the Cassini household. Our home life was set to the rhythm of our parents' mood swings. We shimmied under their radar like dancers under the limbo stick. We understood the difference between going home and coming home.

I routinely spent the first three blocks walking home engaged in imaginary entertainments like dressing our little blond terrier, Tiny Tim, in doll clothes or creating ultimate wish lists. For an entire month I envisioned eating my way through a room packed with columns of neatly stacked fried-bacon strips. The following month, fresh Abba-Zabas replaced the bacon. Subsequently, I imagined diving into a pool of chocolate, and then, my favorite fantasy, baking cookies with June Cleaver.

Rain or shine, I'd swing around stop-sign poles, singing to myself, imitating the toothy-grinned Gene Kelly dancing his way through a rainstorm in *Singin' in the Rain*. Then I'd walk heel to toe along the precarious sidewalk curb that followed Portola Drive along Beresford Creek, where the last of the vacant lots provided year-round access to a flowering bed of sour grass. It was a favorite mid-afternoon snack until Papa told us that every dog on the block pissed on that grass.

Traipsing through the neighborhood with my arms flailing and my mouth sputtering, I was too young to be construed by passersby as abnormal. In my world, sheltered by childhood, Dr. Seuss and I collaborated on my going-home rhyme.

A rhyme in time for little Miss Moan,
Who loved to roam from home to home.
For going home was such a cinch,
Only Mother Dread would have her flinch,
At the thought of going home to the Coming Home Grinch.

When I'd turn the corner at old Mrs. Verber's house on Twenty-Third and Isabelle, I'd invariably feel my pace downshift, muscle memory cautioning me that this was the last block. I'd stop for a moment and peer up the street, squinting in the direction of our house. Like a Native American scout, I was looking for signs of hostile activity. Only the two wagon wheels suspended between the top and bottom rails of our front porch were visible from the corner. Papa's nod to cowboy curb appeal was just one of the many bones of contention my parents had spent the better part of a Fourth of July weekend fighting over. They were like metal on metal. When one rubbed the other the wrong way, sparks flew. We kids stayed out of the crossfire by spotting the early warning signs. Mom's meltdowns ran in six-week cycles. Sometimes the buildup was worse than the blow up. Sometimes the reverse was true. Those two wagon wheels on the porch were like roulette wheels bidding me to take a chance and have a spin before opening the front door.

The best I could hope for was seeing Papa puttering around the front yard. His 2:00 a.m. shift at the garbage company required him to supplement bedtime with an afternoon nap. Papa's naps were sacrosanct; interrupting them could trigger one of Mom's meltdowns. Mom reasoned that yelling "don't wake up your father" at us kids for opening the side door was a necessary precaution. She reasoned this so loudly and for so long, yelling with such venomous, guttural tones and toxic fervor, that invariably Papa would come storming out of their bedroom in his jockey shorts threatening to "use one kid's head to bang the other." Although it was an empty threat, it was full of drastic imagery.

In order to preserve their heads, my sister went to the library after school and my brother played with our cousin next door until dinnertime. I, on the other hand, taught myself to finesse a doorknob open with the stealth precision of a jewel thief. With one ear pinned to the knob, I'd turn it ever so slightly, listening for the subtle tick from the latch indicating that it had recessed sufficiently to clear the door frame. Then I'd inch the door open, again ever so slowly, allowing just enough space for me to enter the hallway leading to my bedroom. I can't say that I was more comfortable in my room, sitting under a veil of silence, listening to Mom talking and laughing to herself. I just wanted to be present when my ultimate wish came true. The wish I had spent all those blocks wishing. I wanted to come home to a normal mother.

The worst-case scenario was walking up the stairs to the front porch and hearing my parents bickering. The living room's big plate-glass window would rattle as the bickering escalated. When it reached a crescendo, Mom would slam the bathroom door behind her and lock herself in for the rest of the evening. By this time, Mom's sister, who lived next door, would arrive.

"What's going on, Primo?"

"Ah, the same ol' thing," Papa would say matter-of-factly. I'd study his face as he buttoned up our coats, searching the creases of his brow for signs of weakness. His jaw was set tight; his fingers worked deliberately but gently in the all-too-familiar act of massaging away my worry. He'd take us down the street to the Pic 'n' Pan, where we'd sit soberly choking down "The Best Hamburgers in Town!" I know Papa thought the place was too expensive for a "hamburg," as he called it.

I don't remember us ever eating at the Pic 'n' Pan with Mom. In fact, we only ate there when Mom had her meltdowns. Maybe it was a restaurant that catered to families in crisis—a sanctuary for kids heavy with the prospect of a broken home. To this day, I've never felt the depth of sadness I felt when I looked across the table at my father's weary face on those occasions. I knew how he felt: the dread at the thought of going home.

❖

Many years later, newly married and living around the corner from my parents, I found myself intercepting my mother one Saturday, talking to herself on her way to warn our fair-haired neighbor. "They're coming to take all the blue-eyed blonds away," my mother said. In my mother's delusional world, she was simply performing an honorable deed on the suggestion of an unseen companion, the one she referred to as "the tall, dark stranger."

A year at Agnew State hospital and a series of electroshock therapy treatments had kept the tall, dark stranger in check for a little over a decade. But now the familiar pattern of random patter and disassociated laughter hinted that mother was entertaining company again.

Mother readily entrusted herself to the young female psychiatrist at the Crisis Intervention Center, the psychiatric emergency facility adjacent to our local hospital. Dr. North was the attending psychiatrist on duty that weekend. She appeared to be in her late twenties, the same age as my sister and I. I remember thinking how young she looked with her clear sharp eyes and open manner—a refreshing change from the lineup of stodgy old male psychiatrists who routinely prescribed medications as if Mom suffered from nothing more than "the vapors."

Schooled in the modern alchemy of psychotropics, Dr. North had access to an arsenal of treatments. I listened intently as she shared her assessment of my mother's mental state: *borderline schizophrenia*. It was the first time I had ever heard a label put to mother's condition.

"Your mother doesn't exactly fit the criteria for this experimental drug," she confided. "But I'm going with my intuition on this one. Let's put it on our wish list."

And so I did—along with dressing the dog in doll clothes, eating my way through a room full of bacon and Abba-Zabas, and diving into a pool of chocolate—right under baking cookies with June Cleaver.

The Huntress and the Leprechauns
By Bardi Rosman Koodrin

MARCH 17, 2013—ST. PADDY'S DAY: my husband Boris and I are celebrating our fortieth wedding anniversary. We're acting every bit like the high school sweethearts we still are.

We've come to a swank Indonesian restaurant in Burlingame, a quaint town near San Francisco. We have a $25 gift certificate in hand and grins on our faces. My *mui mango* margarita comes in the tallest bar glass I've ever seen. Boris is pleased with his huge martini—a dirty something or other. These drinks are *soooo* delicious, we suck down a second round in no time. Fifty-six bucks just for booze? Our coupon has expired? Not the night to be counting pennies—we're celebrating forty years of wedded bliss. Stuffed with spicy Singaporean fare, we charge $138 to our Visa and leave happy.

We find our car. Boris finds his keys. We begin the drive home.

"What's up with the barricades?" I mutter. We realize we've run straight into a sobriety road stop. St. Paddy's Day is a major holiday around here.

A polite policeman sticks his head into our open car window to inquire, "Have you had any alcohol tonight, sir?"

My cordial husband replies, "Why, yes I have officer. I've just had two martinis."

Remember, this restaurant serves tall drinks. I'm happy to be sitting safely in the passenger seat. Then my frame of mind shifts abruptly from the gleeful *tee hee, I'm feeling tipsy* phase to the *oh brother, can I manage it if the cop makes me get out of the car too?* stage.

Worse, I didn't visit the lady's room before we left the restaurant. Unsure of being able to walk straight, I'd feared smashing into the huge Buddha statue standing smack dab in the middle of the aisle. I decided to wait until we got home.

If you've ever been stopped for a drunk test you know it takes a while, given all the nose touching and balancing on one foot—which by the way I can't do on a good day, what with the hole in my head. I have a hydrocephalic cyst on my brain, a fact no cop would believe on a good night. I'd have to push back my hair, reveal the horseshoe scar, and carry on a bit about surviving brain surgery way back when. It's true. They shaved my head, cracked it open like a coconut, and operated on it. I swear it on the old ratty wig shoved in the back of my closet.

Back to my current dilemma. I'm in the car with my right leg bobbing up and down I have to pee so badly. Boris is outside obeying the officer who tells him to walk the line and—Oh! I see a wee leprechaun! No, really. She's wearing an emerald mini-dress with black and white horizontal striped tights; her hair's done up in pigtails tied with big green bows. This leprechaun is having trouble blowing into a Breathalyzer, let alone standing on two legs. The officers holding her upright don't think she's so cute.

After celebrating St. Patrick's Day with Boris for almost fifty years, I can tell you she's not the cutest leprechaun we've come across. We've seen 'em all at various parades and costume parties over the years. Once, on a hiking trail, we encountered a teenaged marching band wearing goofy beards, green jackets, and cocked hats. We never did find out why they were playing their instruments while traipsing through San Bruno's Junipero Serra Park. Then there was the pageant of drag queens adorned in shamrock codpieces and not much else. They were coming down Polk Street on a neon green float, tossing gold foil-wrapped candy coins into the crowd. They passed us just as the Master of Ceremonies Steve Allen, comedian and Tonight Show host, took a swing at Boris instead of the inebriated heckler standing next to him.

After touching on a few of the more memorable St. Paddy's days, my sweetly addled brain is taking me back to the beginning of our personal parade.

❖

During the summer of 1966, the ten girls in my hunting unit had one goal: scoring permanent boyfriends for our junior year of high school at Star of the Sea Academy for Young Ladies. We'd honed our skills with two years of practice boys, but now we'd be upperclasswomen with proms to plan. Most of our summer boys failed to get with the program—a program calling for a selected boy to devote his every thought to the huntress who nabbed him. The ultimate goal was for him to hand over his prized school ring.

We kicked into overdrive in late August. The head honchos of our San Francisco parochial school system provided what they considered appropriate boy/girl interaction in the form of weekly teen club dances with live bands that drew up to two hundred teenagers. The chaperones tried to outsmart us by requiring admission tickets. *Hah.* They seemed clueless about our scalping bids, our ability to climb through bathroom windows, and our bootleg stashes. Seasoned huntresses that we were, my team got into ninety-seven percent of the most popular teen club dances we targeted.

We were thrilled the night we made it into St. Stephen's, the city's number one dance scene featuring a hit teen band, The Vandals. Early on, we lost our team member Dolly, who smelled like a brewery and was captured midway into squeezing through a bathroom window. We saluted our fallen comrade and pushed on. After redoing our hair and applying more layers of makeup, a socially accepted camouflage, we stuck close, scanning for potential marks. We were operating as a unit, yet prepared to go solo at any opportunity. Circling the perimeters of the dance floor at least six times, we ascertained the options and split up into two-girl teams, with Maura acting as a lone scout to track our progress and provide feedback.

My mouth waters thinking of what we could have achieved with today's cell phones, night vision scopes, and GPS capabilities. In 1966, we had only our stealth.

I didn't need any special tools that night. I spotted him clear across the packed room, in one of those magical moments when the din fades and all the other people freeze in mid-motion. This guy took my breath away with his long black hair, dark pensive eyes, broad shoulders, and muscular arms bulging in a navy blue T-shirt.

A distinct voice rang out in my head: *There he is!* My flash reply was: I'm only sixteen—way too young to get serious. The voice rang out again, this time insisting, *There he is!* All right, all right, I muttered to myself. I'll go get him.

He was so buff and tan, with glossy raven hair brushing his broad shoulders, I assumed he was an Apache. My best friend, Kerry, argued he was from the notorious Day Street gang operating out of a rough part of San Francisco. No, I insisted, he's shy, gentle. I did not mention the voice in my head; the unit wouldn't have believed me. Kerry rushed away to collect data. Meanwhile, he was easy to track, remaining solo and stationary.

Kerry soon returned with his credentials: he was from the Sunset District, like me, and entering his senior year at St. Ignatius. He didn't have a girlfriend and he was captain of the football team. *Oh, yes!* The downside, she added with a frown: his name was Boris. *Oh, no!*

Kerry called available unit members to huddle. "Should Bardi go after him or not?"

Donna scanned the room. "I don't see any other girls hanging around him."

Sheila said, "He sure is handsome."

Peggy piped up, "He looks a lot older, though. What if he's in college?"

Fine by me, I thought with a smile. *He's definitely manly enough. And I love his arms.*

Donna frowned, "Maybe she could find someone else?"

Mattie said, "Yeah, I agree."

Not ready to give up without a fight, I challenged, "But why?"

Donna's face turned beet red. "He looks too powerful for a high school guy."

That did it. I wanted him. Besides, maybe Boris had a nickname.

Kerry and I circled him, advancing closer. But suddenly, out of the shadows, the unit's lone scout appeared. Unbeknownst to the rest of us, Maura also had been stalking Boris. We'd forgotten about her! She was ready to pounce. I cringed when she positioned herself so perfectly alongside Boris he had to ask her to dance. Clever girl.

The rules of engagement were clear: Maura had captured the Indian. But we'd never considered what would happen if two huntresses went after the same guy.

The team swore not to inform her of my broken heart.

We'd all pledged to never abandon a rejected teammate while still pursuing our own interests. Kerry went on the prowl and quickly caught me a replacement quarry. She dropped Brent at my feet. Brent was cute and attentive, calling me seven times in two days, but I pined for Boris. Maura gave me a glimmer of hope later in the week when she confessed a glitch in her plan. Boris hadn't asked for her phone number, a crucial possessive step in our *Scoring & Keeping a Boyfriend* manual.

I could hardly wait for the following Saturday's dance. Once we gained entrance, my unit circled the perimeter until we spotted Boris. His Apache mane had been shaved into the buzz-cut necessary for football. Maybe I didn't want him? No, I definitely did. Maura whined that he wasn't as cute anymore. Kerry and I agreed, hoping she'd dump him.

Boris and Maura ended up going out just once. In a strange twist of fate, Brent and I went along as double dates. Boris hardly spoke to me and Maura never did suspect my secret love. I broke up with Brent, an obnoxious child with fast hands, and Maura soon set her sights on a guy named Jim.

I knew Boris was a free agent from my daily surveillance. He was a tough one, remaining shy and wordless at our "chance" meetings. But I refused to give up. Something had changed in me from that first glimpse of him across a crowded room. I was no longer fueled by the energy and tenacity of a resourceful teen acquiring a boyfriend for social activities. My motives were more primal; I'd been innately programmed by the collective consciousness of my female forebears. After Boris, no other man would ever do.

I woke up thirty minutes early each day, transferred buses twice to ride with him to school, tracked his movements across football fields, and showed up every other place he went. My unit assisted by infiltrating his pool of pals. Kerry even claimed a boyfriend she didn't like, though she eventually found another more to her taste.

By then, I'd developed a newfound mature inner strength and knowledge. For six months—an eternity for any love-sick human—my interior voice advised patience, assuring me Boris would eventually get with the program. Finally, I couldn't stand it anymore. I asked him out on our first date, Star of the Sea's St. Patrick's Day Dance, on March 17, 1967.

Six years later to the day, we were married.

Forty-six years later, Boris still takes my breath away. He still looks buff and tan to me, his dark eyes loving and kind. His hair, thinner than it once was, is long again. Now it is a striking silver gray. Boris's version of our love story is that he was stolen as an innocent youth and never had a chance.

I beg to differ. Then again, I was a mighty huntress in those days.

I have a nostalgic grin on my face when Boris gets back into our car. He metabolizes his alcohol well; with a blood level of .02 he's well below the .08 legal limit. I'm halfway tempted to blow into that tube myself, but I have another level of liquid to worry about.

He drives slowly and carefully away from the drunk test area. One block clear, I beg him to step on the gas. "Otherwise," I tell him, "You'll have to rinse out the inside of our car."

"Are you kidding me? After what I just went through?" He knows that the San Mateo police have little else to do than look for the very thing I'm begging my designated driver to do: speed down El Camino on St. Paddy's night.

With my right leg bob-bob-bobbing to the beat of a Led Zeppelin classic blasting away on the radio, we're quite the forty-year-married couple out on the town, even if it is driving within the limits through the quiet tree-lined streets of Burlingame, Millbrae, and home sweet home, San Bruno. We've arrived at our little blue house nestled between two parks.

Boris pulls into our driveway. I've already unstrapped my seatbelt for a quick exit from the car. I have my house keys in hand for my run to the bathroom.

As I clutch the car door handle, a glint of silver catches my eye.

Some husbands buy their wives diamond rings. My husband surprises me with rings shaped like raptors. On my left hand is a stately owl. My right sports a silver hawk with wings expanded.

Even in my current state of urgency, I can't help but smile.

I am a mighty huntress!

Tender Years in the Tenderloin
By Jo Carpignano

DOWNTOWN SAN FRANCISCO was a pretty quiet place in the 'seventies. The political and social turmoil of the 'sixties had died down. The beat generation was wearing thin and the hippies had either grown up or given up. Those who had given up were identified as street people. They slept on sidewalks and lined up for free meals at Glide Memorial. Working the system was a way of life, and it was all I knew at age twelve.

We lived on Larkin Street, a few blocks north of Market in a third-floor walkup apartment with two rooms. There were four chairs and a table in the bigger room and a bed, a cot, and a dresser in the other. The single small bathroom held an old tub and a sink. The place was a pig sty. Ma didn't think picking up dirty diapers was worth the bother, since another would follow within a short time.

Ma was a single parent and we were on welfare. At thirty-two, she already had four kids, with another on the way. I was the oldest, so it was my job to look out for my two younger brothers. Two-year-old Emily was just learning to walk.

Ma grew impatient as her belly got bigger by the day. The rooms were big, but too many of us filled the space.

"The more the merrier," Charlie would claim on his weekly visits. We heard that this was his routine comment with the other families, too. He would visit, bring groceries, and collect Ma's welfare money. He'd stick around for a few hours when he was in the mood. He and Ma would go to the bedroom and lock the door. We kids would ignore the noise and turn up the TV. That was okay with me. But I don't think Ma was happy. She came out of the bedroom a tousled mess, grumpy and mean for the rest of the day.

She was grumpy and mean even when Charlie wasn't around. I was eager to leave for school every morning as soon as I could get my two little brothers dressed and out the door. There was a hot breakfast waiting for us at school, and that was okay with me too.

Weekends were not so easy. By the end of the week, the good breakfast food had run out, so oatmeal was the usual for us on weekends. Three times a day on Saturday and sometimes on Sunday too, if Charlie didn't show up.

One Sunday morning, I got snippy with Ma about eating oatmeal all the time. She didn't like it at all.

"You damn brat, what do you mean you don't *like* oatmeal? How would you like it if there wasn't no oatmeal? Huh? How would you like that!" she bellowed. "You know what? You don't get to eat no oatmeal today, missy, that's what! If you don't like oatmeal, you can stand over there by the door and watch us eat oatmeal."

I froze and refused to move away from the table. That only made her madder. She stood up from her chair, reached out, and slapped me across the face.

"You do what I say, when I say!" She clenched her teeth and pushed me off my chair. "You stand against the wall, right by the door, jus' like I said."

I went to the wall, my cheek burning, and stood by the door as I'd been told. Ma was fuming and stumbling as she returned to her chair. She sat down at the table with the other kids eating *their* oatmeal, silent and watchful. It had been the wrong time for me to complain.

She's been drinking again, I thought. I'd forgotten that Charlie'd brought a bottle with the last delivery.

I stood and waited, hoping my silence would keep Ma from another angry outburst. Instead, she smiled, but it was not a happy smile.

"So, you're tired of eating oatmeal? Well then, let's see if *this* is better for you."

She scooped a spoonful of oatmeal from the bowl, turned, and flung it at me from across the room. Her aim was perfect. The oatmeal hit my shoulder.

"Is that better now? If you don't want to eat it, you can wear it. Okay?"

A second spoonful landed on my forehead and a third on my chest. I cried while my brothers looked on, fascinated by the oatmeal assault.

Just then the door swung open, pushing me aside, and Charlie walked in. I was never so pleased to see him arrive.

"What the hell is going on here?" he demanded.

"The brat got tired of *eating* oatmeal," my mother explained, "so she's gonna wear it instead."

"Well, goddamn, woman, you gonna turn her into a oatmeal statue, you keep this up." He started to laugh.

Ma quit throwing the oatmeal and started laughing too. My two brothers started to laugh along with them. Everyone was laughing except for me. I was still crying.

"Well, you stupid kid, go get cleaned up!" Ma yelled.

"Hold up there, honey, let me help get that mess offa you," Charlie offered.

I finally found my voice. "No! I can do it! No, Charlie. Thanks anyways."

I turned quickly into the bathroom and shut the door behind me, giving in to my tearful humiliation. I never complained about oatmeal again.

Charlie must have felt sorry for me that Sunday because he was awfully nice to me the rest of the morning. He thanked me for helping him bring some of the groceries up from his car and talked to me about how sorry he was that Ma got so mad at me.

"You know that baby's due in a few months, and she's jus' about wore out with takin' care of Emily. Don't know what's wrong with that li'l one. She don' seem so quick as your brothers were at two year. You jes' gotta he'p your ma the bes' you can, 'til the baby gets born."

I wasn't sure what Charlie thought I could do, any more than what I already was doing with taking care of Tom and Jimmy. And I was not really looking forward to another baby.

"What if things get worse after the baby comes? What then?" I asked.

"Why, honey, we get the social worker out here, and find somebody to help out. 'Sides, the welfare check will be bigger and we can do some things to make it easier for your ma."

So that's why Charlie was so eager for the baby to arrive, I thought. *The welfare check would get bigger.*

In the meantime, I was to continue taking care of my two brothers, who attended the same school as I did. Jimmy was not so bad. He was in second grade and keeping up with the other kids in his class. He liked his teacher and got along well with everybody. Tom was another story. His fifth grade teacher was always telling me how he was fighting with other kids.

"He just doesn't seem to be able to get along with others. He insists on being first all the time, even when they play games. And that's not how we do things, you know," Mrs. Brown complained.

"Sorry, Mrs. Brown. I'll talk to him about taking turns," I apologized.

In a much more serious tone, Mrs. Brown said, "I really don't think that's your job, Nadine. This is not the first time you've tried to help. Your mother needs to be dealing with this problem. Do you think you could ask her to come to school for a conference sometime soon?"

I took a deep breath and tried to think of something that would explain why Ma could never make it to any school conference. If she got a report about Tom being so bad the teacher had to see her about it, Ma would get out that wooden spoon and make Tom all black and blue again.

"Well, you know, my mother is going to have a baby soon, and I'm not sure she could walk all that way in her condition."

John Muir Elementary School was a good six or eight blocks from where we lived, so I wasn't telling a lie. Ma could never walk that far now.

"Couldn't she take a bus or get a ride from someone?" Mrs. Brown suggested.

"No ma'am, there's no money for bus fare, and Ma don't have any friends with cars. I'll tell her about Tom, and she will talk to him about being good, 'specially on the playground."

I hoped this would satisfy Mrs. Brown, and that she would let me take care of it again. But Mrs. Brown was not to be satisfied by the assurances of a twelve year old.

"I think I'll talk to her on the phone, then," she said.

"But we don't have a phone," I answered quickly. "And I'm sure that when I tell her how serious the problem is, Ma will find a way to help Tom straighten out."

"Oh, you don't have a phone."

Mrs. Brown seemed to be running out of options, and I was hoping that she would settle for my latest suggestion. But not Mrs. Brown. She was determined to make that parent contact, and though I'd been able to *deflect* her other attempts (I'd just learned the word *deflect* in a book I read), she found another possibility.

"Well, then, I think I'd better consult with Miss Gray and see if we can think of another way," she concluded as she walked away.

My heart sank. Miss Gray, the principal, was a formidable woman (I just learned the word *formidable* too). Between the two of them, there was not a chance that I'd be able to protect Tom from another thrashing.

Early Monday morning, the boys were about ready for school and I was collecting my finished homework from the table. Ma was in the bathroom with Emily. I spotted her purse on the chair. She usually kept it in the bedroom in the bottom drawer. But I guessed that she was short on cigarettes and planned to go out as soon as Tom, Jimmy, and I were gone. So the purse was there ready for her to grab as soon as we were out the door and Emily was cleaned up.

I don't know what made me do it, but I knew how to be quick, too. The coin purse was just inside the first section of the handbag. I opened the clip, grabbed a coin, and slipped it into my pocket. The coin purse went back in the bag. Nothing looked different.

"'Bye Ma!" I said as I herded the two boys out the door and down the stairs. We were on the sidewalk in no time, hustling towards the school.

"I saw what you did," Tom said softly.

"What did she do?" asked Jimmy, oblivious as usual to what was going on around him. Sometimes I thought he was trying not to know, and that was okay with me.

"She took money outa Ma's pocketbook," Tom explained.

"Wow, are you gonna get in trouble when Ma finds out," Jimmy added.

"And how's she gonna find out?" I asked.

"Well, I bet she knows how much money she had in that little purse, and if she don't remember, I'm gonna tell," Tom warned.

"Now why would you wanna do that?" I asked. "You think she's gonna do you a favor for tellin' on me?"

"Maybe not, but you boss us around all the time. I think maybe it would be fun to see what happens when Ma knows you's stealin' from her purse."

"Naw! Come on, Tommy, don' tell, don' tell," Jimmy interrupted.

This argument was getting really serious. I thought I'd better do something pretty quick or we'd all be in trouble.

"Well, let's see how much I have and what we can do with it."

I reached into my pocket and came out with the dime I had taken.

"Hey, look here, a whole dime. What do you think we can buy with a dime, you guys? Got any ideas?"

"Ain't nothin' much we can get with that," Tom offered hesitantly. But now he was using *we* instead of *you*, so there was progress in the right direction. I'd known Tom from when he was a baby, and it had always been easy to find ways to get him interested if there was something for him involved.

"How about on our way home from school we stop at the corner store and see if we can find something we all like. Then we can share," I offered.

And so the conspiracy was formed (I liked the word *conspiracy*).

After school we stopped at the store, bought a pack of gum, and chewed happily all the way home. We found a clean spot on the frame of the apartment door and parked our gum there, ready to pick up the following morning. It gave us all something to look forward to, I thought.

When we walked in the door of our apartment, I could see that Ma had her new pack of Lucky Strikes and was smoking away. She didn't say a word about missing money from her purse.

Tom kept his silence. Jimmy was the good boy he always was and I got away with getting something I wanted for myself. Even if I did have to share.

Color My World
By Ellen Six

"MOTHER, TODAY IN CATECHISM CLASS I learned that God made everyone and that we are all God's children."

Mother dismissed my pronouncement. "That's fine," she said. "Now go do your school work."

I grew up in a racially divided city. Chicago had its boundaries. One side of a main street was white and the other side was black. The word *black* would have been an insult to African Americans back then, as the only words used for race at the time were *white* and *colored*.

On rent day, our tenant stopped by to talk to Mother. He expressed a fear I had heard voiced frequently. "They are coming closer," he said, and mentioned main streets like Halsted, Loomis, and Western Avenue. Whole neighborhoods would change if a Negro family moved in. Whites would flee to the suburbs if they could afford it.

I listened in on the adult conversation. It had not really registered with me previously, but this time, with my new knowledge from catechism class, I interjected, "Sister says that we should love everyone because God made all people."

Startled, the tenant looked at me, an impudent kid usually hiding behind her mother's skirts, and shot back an answer.

"Sure, love all people. But those Negroes are not people, they are animals."

Mother gave me that stern look that said, "Be quiet."

Once he left, she gave me a lecture about respecting my elders and keeping my foolish ideas to myself. Mother, who had been raised in Lithuania, had never seen a race other than white until she came to America. At first, she thought that a dark-skinned person had a bad sunburn or that an Asian had squinted too long at the sun. These were not people she had ever met or gotten to know. They were just "them." Like our tenant, she was caught up in the fear of falling property values if "they" moved any closer. "They" were thought of as an enemy who could steal away your dream of home ownership and seen as an abiding threat. She ended her lecture, insisting that she was right and some people were, indeed, better than others.

"Now, Elyte, go study your school work. And no more foolish ideas."

Books were part of my life from first grade through my first days of college. I went to University to become an English teacher. This career made sense for a girl who spent her childhood reading books from one end of the library shelf to the other.

My first class in English Composition was a make-or-break course. The professor would randomly pull a student's paper from the pile on his desk and proceed to point out the errors while mocking the student's writing style. It was a stomach-churning exercise. The one good thing that came of this experience was that we students formed an instant connection. Anyone could become the next target.

After one such class, four of us girls bonded as we waited for the elevator. We decided to head to Walgreens to lament the situation and release our tensions over coffee. English class and survival coffee became our weekly ritual. One Lithuanian girl, one Polish girl, one Irish girl, and a beautiful blond model. We became a sisterhood born of stress.

One Monday, the blond member wanted our advice. The fraternity president had asked her to attend a fraternity dance as his date. He told her that with her good looks and charm, she might even be crowned queen. Our shrieks of delight could be heard all the way to the Water Tower across the street on Michigan Avenue. Of course she should go to the dance! Without a doubt she would be queen! Why was she hesitating?

She feared that the boy would not want to date her if he really knew about her. "Knew what?" we asked. That she was smart, and talented, and beautiful?

"He wouldn't want to date me if he knew I was a Negro," she said.

We sat stunned. She was blond and had a lighter complexion than any of us.

She told us about her family background and produced an I.D. card. The line designating race read "Negro."

We assured her it wouldn't matter. But as I rode the EL train back home that evening, I tried to understand my feelings about her revelation. Now, she, my friend, was one of "them." In an instant, a wall had gone up between us. I awoke after a restless night wondering how I could deal with this new knowledge. The world I grew up in was either black or white. Boundaries were set; one didn't cross lines. Yesterday she was my friend. What was she today? I decided that she was my friend yesterday and she would be my friend today. Nothing would change.

The four of us continued to meet for coffee every Monday to de-stress. We later learned that she had turned down the fraternity president's invitation without explanation.

Do we need—did we ever need—to set boundaries between "them" and "us"? For me, the question has been answered.

Just ask my Asian son-in-law.

A Hummingbird's Tune
By Martha Clark Scala

She is playing a fiddle in her head
the bow stretched with taut strings.
Her body listens,
wonders,
where the wound will go next
as a hummingbird flits from
feeder to feeder.
She seeks blessed oil of anointment,
a lantern of light
that points and leads
out of dark spaces.

She is more than ready
to pluck a different tune
toss the bow into a campfire
where Girl Scouts savor s'mores
and sing,
their joyful melody
filling empty caverns,
those rooms in that house,
a house large enough
for mercy and grace
but lacking.

Premonition
By Amy Kelm

MONA WEEKLY KNEW she was dying the moment she opened her eyes. The pain shooting through her abdomen was sharp and specific. She grimaced and tried to sit up in bed. "Ouch," she said softly. She doubled over, pressing both hands into her stomach to ease the pain. This was it. The end.

Funny, she hadn't felt anything the night before. She'd felt great all week. She'd turned forty on Sunday and had been treated to non-stop birthday celebrations by friends and doting family, culminating last evening with a trip to the much-anticipated *L'Etoile,* an exquisite new French restaurant in downtown Madison. The food was rich and every bit as scrumptious as she'd imagined. She'd savored every morsel of cheese put in front of her, drank more *vin* than she ought to have, and gobbled *coq au vin* before finishing with a decadent *mousse au chocolat.* It was lovely. She'd even licked the bowl in defiance of her newly realized middle-aged status.

But now she was dying. It was a shame. She'd have liked to visit the restaurant again.

"Shit," she said to no one but herself. "Today of all days." It really was inconvenient. It was only Wednesday. There was still so much of the week ahead of her. This morning she had to get the kids out the door to school and run some errands she'd been neglecting. This afternoon she'd have to tend to the kids' never-ending series of activities. Both Susan and Cole had soccer *and* band practice that afternoon and she was on deck for the carpool. Why she'd ever agreed to this schedule was beyond her. How would she ever fit anything else in today, let alone dying? Plus, the forecast called for beautiful weather. No one should die on a sunny day.

She limped slowly into the kitchen; the searing pain subsided. What a relief. She needed time to make lunches and get the kids out the door. She could die after she made peanut butter and honey for Susan and grilled cheese for Cole. Then she'd need to put the dishes in the dishwasher and wipe down the counters. She wouldn't want to leave her house a mess. What would the neighbors think? People would certainly stop by to offer condolences. Maybe even bring casseroles. She hoped there was room in the freezer. Her dear husband Geoffrey would be too grief-stricken to clean, so she might as well do it herself. Maybe vacuum, too. She wouldn't want the last impression of her to be that she was a slob.

Mona sighed. Dying was going to take more effort than she wanted to expend today. Too bad this couldn't have happened on Friday—after the cleaners had come.

"Oh..." Mona gasped and doubled over. The pain in her abdomen that was surely killing her had returned. Cancer? She clutched the counter top. This time the pain lasted much longer than it had earlier that morning, surely signaling the end. Her body stiffened and she held her breath for the roughly eight seconds it took to pass.

"Are you okay, Mom?" asked Cole, looking up from his toasted waffles.

Her ten-year-old was such a sweet and sensitive boy, always expressing concern while the rest of the family seemed indifferent to matters of health. "I'm fine, honey. Don't worry about me. Just eat your breakfast," Mona reassured him. "I'm sure this is nothing. And chew those waffle pieces carefully. I may have cut them a little too big."

"Morning, honey," said Geoffrey, walking briskly into the kitchen. "What do you have going on today?" He paused to kiss her on the cheek and continued past on his way to grab coffee.

"Mom's sick," said Cole, drizzling circles of syrup onto his plate.

"Oh, it's nothing," Mona said.

"It didn't look like nothing. You were all hunched over," Cole continued.

"Don't talk with your mouth full, sweetheart. And wipe up that syrup from the table. You're dripping all over."

Geoffrey grabbed a bagel from the toaster, sat down, and began reading the paper. "I can't believe the Brewers lost again last night! I was sorry we couldn't make it to the game but it looks like we didn't miss much."

"I'm sure I'll be fine," said Mona. "It was just a crazy strange pain that stabbed me in the stomach. I couldn't breathe for a few minutes, but it passed."

"Uh-huh," Geoffrey mumbled, continuing to scan the sports section. "With that loss they're under 500! Can you believe it? Good thing the rest of the division stinks. They may still have a chance to pull something out before the All-Star Break." He flipped the paper to the next page. "I'm sorry, honey. You said your stomach was hurting? Do you think you should go see someone?"

"Oh, I don't know." Mona found comfort in her husband's concern. A validation that he would, in fact, miss her when she was gone. "I suppose I should. I have lots of errands to run, though. You know how it is. Today after I get the kids off to school, I have to get the dry cleaning and take those boxes to the post office. And I really should clean out the freezer."

"The freezer?" asked Geoffrey, without looking up.

"Oh, you know how overcrowded it can get. And you never know when you're going to need the space..." Her voice trailed off. It was too much to think about. Plus, her family hated casseroles. What would they eat after she was gone and there was no one to cook for them?

Geoffrey got up. "Well, you call me if you need me." He bent slightly to kiss her on the forehead and grabbed his briefcase. "See you tonight," he said, waving over his shoulder.

"Yes," she called after him. "See you... um... tonight. And honey, drive carefully."

❖

Mona finished shooing her kids off to school and phoned her doctor. She knew calling for same-day appointments was frowned upon, but she hoped they would make an exception for a dying woman.

Mona sat at her desk and listened patiently to the hold music. She opened her computer and pulled up the exercise schedule at the gym. It had been four days since her last workout. She really should try to get one in today, especially after last night's dinner. It might even take her mind off the impending doom—if anything could take your mind off something like that. Would the tumor growing in her stomach make exercise difficult?

Thankfully, she hadn't felt anything in the past twenty minutes or so. Maybe it wasn't cancer. If she chose a short class—or maybe one not quite as hard as usual—she might be able to manage it. Water aerobics could be an option...

The receptionist finally came back on the line. "I really need to see someone today," Mona said. "I'm having terrible pains in my abdomen." She began answering the receptionist's questions. "Yes. Mona Weekly. 5-30-73. My doctor? Dr. Gates. What time? Nine-thirty or eleven? Let's see, I'll take the eleven. Yes. See you then. Thank you."

Eleven was perfect. It gave her just enough time to get to the gym, take a class, shower, and drive to the doctor's office. She stood up to get ready.

"Owww!" Mona grimaced. There it was again. Death. Back with a vengeance. Momentarily unable to move, she braced one hand against each wall of the hallway and closed her eyes. When the pain dissipated roughly five seconds later, Mona hurried back to begin changing. "Shit," she spat again. She would need to shave before putting her swimsuit on.

Exhausted and sporting wet hair, Mona rushed into the doctors' office at 11:02 a.m. She had been in such a hurry that she skipped grabbing a cup of free coffee at the gym, though she hated to miss that brilliant jolt of caffeine. Normally, she would have downed three cups of the liquid gold by this time. But today she hadn't even had one. Dying will do that. It messes *everything* up.

Mona waited patiently until her name was called and then followed the nurse into the exam room, where she changed into the paper smock and crawled up on the table.

Why was this happening? Why now? She was too young to die, wasn't she? It wasn't fair. How could she leave her beautiful children? They were still so small. They needed her. How would they get along without her? Geoffrey's temper was short and she knew he'd be a mess. Would he remarry? He should, the poor man. She *must* remember to tell him that he should remarry. The kids would benefit from having a woman in the house. But Geoffrey must be picky. Not just *any* woman should be allowed to care for *her* kids. Certainly not that divorcée from school, Lee-Anne. She'd have to remember to warn Geoffrey about Lee-Anne. *That* woman was trouble of the worst kind. Mona had heard that Lee-Anne regularly sent her kids to school without water bottles. And she never volunteered without being asked *twice*. Maybe Geoffrey could find someone from church, someone who would know how to French-braid Susan's hair. Yes, that was important. Her beautiful little girl... Maybe she should take Susan to get her hair cut after school. A chin-length bob would be cute. Susan could even manage that style herself.

The doctor's knock startled her. "Hello, Mrs. Weekly. How are you?" said Dr. Gates.

Mona tried to be brave but she heard her voice quiver. "Oh, you know... I'm not that great, actually."

"I see from the chart that you're having some pain in your abdomen. Please lie down."

Mona obeyed and stared up at the ceiling tiles. Fear swirled around her head and coursed through her veins, grabbing every cell in her body. Tears formed in the corners of her eyes. She didn't want to die.

Dr. Gates quietly pushed and prodded her from multiple angles before asking her to sit up. "Mrs. Weekly, when was your last BM?"

"Oh," said Mona, startled and embarrassed by the unexpected question. "Um...maybe, Monday. It could have been Sunday. Or Saturday But I think it was Monday."

"I see. I think that's it, Mrs. Weekly. *You're constipated.* I can feel that you're backed up in there," he said with a slight smile. "The pains you're feeling are likely gas pains. Have you had anything especially rich to eat in the past few days?"

"Well, now that you mention it, yes."

"Let's try a laxative, Mrs. Weekly. And lots of water." Dr. Gates stood and handed her a prescription. "Try this one. It's very gentle. If you're still having pain in forty eight hours, give me a call back."

Mona sat dumbfounded as Dr. Gates closed the door behind him. *Of course.* Why hadn't she put two and two together? She exhaled loudly. Her shoulders fell back to their regular position and Mona sat straighter than she had all day. She swung her legs over the side of the table and jumped to the floor. She dressed quickly and paused to admire her now-dry hair in the mirror. She looked pretty good for forty!

Keys in hand, Mona whistled as she bounced toward her car. Life was good. No, life was *great*. What should she make for dinner? Fettuccini Alfredo? Or maybe she should try that new stroganoff recipe she'd cut out of the magazine. Geoffrey would love—

She stopped abruptly in the middle of the parking lot and grabbed her head. The dull pain she'd been feeling all morning behind her eyes had materialized into a full-blown headache. A *terrible* headache. She'd been too preoccupied with dying to pay it much attention, but now it was throbbing wildly across the very front of her head, impossible to escape.

"Oh, no!" Mona closed her eyes and rubbed her temples. "An aneurism."

Amethyst
By Diane Lee Moomey

NOW I KNOW WHERE YOU LIVE and where you sleep: curled up in a deep corner of what I like to call my mind. You have your own room here, your books and your music. You have always lived here. Fifteen years ago, ten years ago, I cursed those tendrils of your thought that wrapped themselves around mine. Today, I know you did not choose this, either. You simply live here. We both live here; we woke up in this space and call it home. Today, in my forty-fifth year, I call it good. My friends and I talk of boundaries, a popular topic these days—mapping out territories thus and so: *you* may come this far, *you* have to stay over there, *I* will not step over this line. These boundaries are chalk on the pavement, fences made of water. These boundaries do not exist. I know this is true because you are here.

Tonight, three thousand miles away, I feel you stir in your sleep. You turn so the arthritic hip is not so squarely under you and try to find a soft place in which to settle its ache. Your hands! So pale now, so delicate, it breaks my heart to look at them. I feel the amethyst ring on your finger, the ring your mother gave to you when you were eighteen, that her mother gave to her when she was eighteen, that you did not give to me when I was eighteen. I cannot blame you for this. Your mother was newly dead when I was eighteen and you chose to keep that crumb of her life—all you had left. I cannot blame you for this. I was a wild girl. I might have lost the ring and that would have been more than you could have borne. I cannot blame you, but my heart aches for something unfinished. I am the daughter *manquée*, the one not part of the ring chain.

We live here. We have always lived here, though I have *not* always known this. For twenty five years I lived the comfortable fiction that I was alone in the house of my own mind, that it was *my* house. One day in my twenty-sixth year, fiction crumbled and I saw, with perfect angry clarity, *you*. Here.

You must remember that day. I had been staying with you at the cottage. My brother, your son, your sun, had met us there. We'd visited.

"I'll drive you home," he'd said. "No need to take the train—I'll drop you in Toronto on my way back to Chicago." You made a package of food for our trip: a kind act of sandwiches, apples, cookies you had baked yourself. And thermoses of coffee—you made those for us, too.

My brother and I drove away, waving as we always have. We sat in silence for half a mile until I began to feel a dull brown buzzing inside my head, all too familiar. I did what I have always done with that feeling: babble until it goes away. I began to babble of coffee, of how I love to have coffee in bed first thing in the morning. Coffee: French Roast, Sumatra, fresh ground, cream, more cream, nutmeg. My brother, your son, stopped the car, turned around in his seat, peeled away layers of jackets, blankets, garment bags, paper bags, plastic bags.

"Our coffee!" he cried. "We forgot the coffee!"

We retraced our drive. You stood on the porch, smiling and waving the thermoses, one in each hand. You cried out.

"When I saw you had forgotten these, I sat down and closed my eyes and thought hard, 'Diane, your coffee! Diane, your coffee!'"

You were delighted. I was livid. I smiled stiffly and said "thank you" as a daughter should. Livid because *now I knew, and I could never go back to not knowing*. The wrath was not about coffee messages, but about trespass. *You have trespassed, have always trespassed and now I know it clearly, no doubts*. All the energy I must have expended in my young life, pushing away your wishes! At that instant I knew it all, and would not forgive you for making me know.

That was twenty years ago. Twenty years have rubbed us smooth, clean, round. Wrath has ebbed away. Today, you no longer push at me, no longer poke fingers into my corners. Perhaps my father, your husband, now fills your attention with the needs of his faltering body, or you may

105

have no energy to spare, or you may be old enough and wise enough to see that it is not worth your effort to try rolling my stone uphill. Whatever the reason, today you are simply here and nothing more. I live with you as with an old roommate. The sharp edges are gone and we no longer fret about who left the cap off the toothpaste.

And when you die, when your body crumples and stops working? Ah. I do not want to think about that. My life as I know it will end because your awareness will become something else. It may stop, it may migrate to a place beyond my ability to reach, it may do something unimaginable, but *this* I know as surely as I know that dust settles: I will no longer be I. The "I" of today, the "I" my friends love, the "I" my lover loves, the "I" that I love, will become something else. I fear this.

Perhaps this is why people have children, to keep the bottle of Self full to overflowing, so when Mother is no longer, DaughterSon are already within, their own rooms furnished and lived in. But I have no children, no beings of my own flesh, no young one whose cells I share.

So, when you die—

But you are not so very old, even now. Your family's women are tough. They live long; they do well in their bodies. Thirty years may pass before I need to touch the fact of your death. I may have thirty years to prepare for that which cannot be prepared for.

Tonight, again, I turn lightly to the place where you stay, feel it with my mind's fingers. You are restless—that hip bothers you still. You feel scratchy, irritable; your day has been filled with unfinished business, with small nuisance spats with my father, your husband. You have lost weight again and the amethyst ring is loose on your finger. You turn it around and around in the hollow spot between the knuckles, think of your own mother and of how you did not know her well enough. You turn the ring and think of me, who will wear it someday. You hope that we *will* know each other well enough. You turn the ring again.

I put away my books, my journal, and turn back the covers.

Good night.

My lover sleeps, bearlike. You turn your face away; you do not pry. Discreet—you are discreet.

I turn out the light.

The Outback
By James Hanna

TWO DROVERS WERE CAMPED in a dense grove of fig trees. While the shorthorns grazed on a swath of Mitchell grass, the men rested on their swags. A dingo watched them from the edge of the grove.

Jim Cooper, a rangy stockman with a squint, poked a stick at the billycan as though urging it to come to a boil. But the crackle of the scrubwood was faint and unpromising. A livelier sound came from the flying foxes high overhead—a thick cloud of rat-sized rodents, which, at a distance, looked almost like birds.

Tom Hemmings brushed at the flies dotting his face and gazed at the dingo. The animal unnerved him, he had to admit. Although comely and small, with permanently cocked ears, it exhibited none of the sociability he associated with dogs. Its gaze was opportunistic, not fawning, and it appeared to have taken measure of the rifle in Jim's hand, a .30-06 Remington he had pulled from the scabbard on his saddle.

"They're little yellow bah-sterds," Jim muttered, removing a slim cartridge from his hip pocket and coaxing it into the breach. "Only bugger I know of who will ravage without good cause. In Queensland they put up special fences to keep 'em away from the sheep, but it don't do much good. The buggers know how to dig under fences. And they'll wipe out a flock of sheep just for bloody sport."

"Are there bounties on them?" Tom asked. He suspected the question was naïve, but he was determined to learn all he could about the Northern Territory of Australia, his new homeland since dropping out of Stanford six months ago. The land was so stark and irrepressible that it would never attain statehood.

"There are in Queensland," Jim said. "A dingo scalp there fetches a hundred quid in some parts. But in the Territory they can run amok for all anyone seems to care."

"That speaks well for the Territory," Tom said. "They put up with mongrels here."

Jim grinned. "They do at that. But a dingo ain't a mongrel. A pure-bred devilment is what he is." He released the safety and sighted the long barrel in the direction of the dingo. The animal, as though charmed, continued to watch them. Dissatisfied with the range, Jim lowered the rifle to his lap.

"So what were you doing in Sydney?" he asked. "Catching up on your rooting?"

"I did lose my cherry there," Tom said, a dubious boast for a twenty-one-year-old man. But he hoped the turn in conversation would distract Jim from the dingo. Tom did not want the animal shot.

"Good on ya," Jim said. "You'll have Buckley's chance of it in the Territory—not with twenty blokes for every blooming sheila here. Course, you could get a bit on the reservations—if you don't mind jockeying a darkie, that is. The lubras will do you there for a swig of plock, they will."

"Have you spent much on plock?"

"Haven't lately," Jim chuckled. "But I have jockeyed me share of 'em. Can't say it did me any harm either. There's not much that separates strumpets, you know. They're about all the same in the dark."

Tom sighed deeply. He envied Jim's devil-may-care attitude—a perverse inner harmony to which he could only aspire. His companion in Sydney, a prostitute named Jenny, had not been so easy for him to dismiss. He regretted missing her as much as he did, yet he found her memory more sustaining than her company had been. With the practical gaze of a hustler, she had looked without sentiment into his soul.

"You're wild, Thomas," she had told him one day. "And that's really all that can be said about it. Not that you seem that way, mind you. You're as skinny as a bloody boong and I doubt that you know how to make love at all. But that really doesn't change matters, does it? A law unto yourself, you are, and as wild as the blooming sea."

He had parted company with her on a rainy morning several weeks before arriving in the Territory, as abruptly as he had once burned his draft card. He had left her asleep in a King's Cross boarding house, not wishing to wake her. They had argued the day before and he did not wish to renew the argument. But he had sent her his address at Birdstone Cattle Station and, in spite of himself, looked forward to the arrival of the weekly mailbag from Darwin. She had told him once that she wrote to servicemen in Vietnam, so he hoped she would be as charitable to him.

The dingo yawned as the billycan steamed. Jim put down the rifle. Moving awkwardly, he dangled the billy from a twig and carried it to his tucker-bag. After smothering the steam with a fistful of tea leaves, Jim stirred the concoction with a swirl of his finger and set it aside to brew.

"I don't do well with women," Tom blurted. "They're too damn clingy."

"Women," Jim spat. "They're more trouble than they're worth, if ya ask me. The palm of your hand will do you no worse a job and you won't end up catching the clap from it." He yanked two tin cups from the tucker-bag and set them upright on the ground. The billy he handled more carefully, pinching the base with a rag to avoid being singed by the scalding metal. He filled only one of the cups before setting the billy back on the ground. Squatting back down, he sipped cautiously at the hot tea.

"It's a fair dinkum life here without 'em," he said. "If you can handle the heat and the flies. Good place for a draft dodger, anyhow. The authorities won't hunt a bloke down in the Never Never. Wouldn't be much point to it, would there?"

"Have you given them a reason?" Tom asked. Watching the ambivalence with which Jim sipped the tea, he decided he did not want any.

Jim nodded. "I have at that," he said. "Had a bit of a donnybrook in a Darwin pub last month and they hauled me in front of the magistrate. But he cut me loose the same day, he did. Said I coulda gone to Fannie Bay Jail, but they needed it for the boongs."

"Was it over a woman?"

"No fear," Jim replied. "What I done was punch a little Englishman who let his mouth override his arse. 'Stead of standing me a beer when it was over, like any gentleman woulda done, the pommy bah-sterd went to the cop shop and pressed charges. Cost me a pretty quid, he did, but I'm not saying it wasn't worth it." He shrugged like a martyr and shook his head stoically. He took another sip of the tea. "But I did get locked up in Brisbane. Spent two years in the Boggo Road Jail. That seems as far back as the Dreamtime, it does."

"That's a lot for a brawl," Tom muttered. He spoke angrily, perhaps because the Outback, with its endless expanse of mudflats, bull dust, and crocodile-infested swamps, had forged an uncommon bond between them—a willingness, on behalf of either, to honor the misadventures of the other.

"Guess I showed 'em me arse." Jim laughed. "Rape of a minor, they called it, but a fair go is what it was—a little Tasmanian tart who lied about her age. She did five other blokes the same night she had me, then tried to charge me a tenner for stirring sloppy seconds. Ran straight to the cop shop when I wouldn't cough it up."

Tom nodded with genuine sympathy, not doubting for a moment the merit of Jim's story and the shortsightedness of the judge who had taken his liberty. That Jim's liberty was a shoddy affair—a continuum of whoring, drunkenness, and cattle rustling—did not devalue it in the slightest.

Jim finished the tea with a heavy gulp and tossed the wet dregs on the ground. "My oath," he remarked, "it's a fair dinkum life out here. If a bloke don't go troppo, that is."

Shaking his head, Jim picked the rifle back up. He blew sharply upon the muzzle, clearing the dust from the sight— an extravagant gesture since the dingo was no longer visible. Removing a soiled handkerchief from his pocket, he began to wipe the barrel clean.

"It appears he lucked out."

"Would you want to wager on it?" Jim said. "I'm bettin' a quid I get a shot off yet. They're persistent little buggers when they get a notion into their heads."

Soon the barrel was gleaming, spitting off sunlight. Jim cradled it lovingly. His attention to the weapon seemed almost licentious—a reminder to Tom that Outback dwellers were all a little crazy. What troubled Tom, however, was not Jim's eccentricity so much as his own desire to emulate him.

Watching Jim stroke the rifle, caressing it as though it were a lover, Tom was reminded of the extent of his own displacement. He remembered an old couple with grandchildren in New South Wales who had picked him up on the Pacific Highway after the Land Rover he bought in Sydney broke down. They had taken him to their home, a large bungalow in Lismore, where he had stayed for less than a day. They had wanted him to stay longer, but the strain of making conversation had been too high a price to pay for clean sheets and warm food. He had left the next day before sunrise and hitchhiked to Brisbane, where he had hired on with the Birdstone Cattle Corporation. He remembered the utter relief of returning to the open road. The paradox of his departure—that he found less to be missed in empty spaces—had not escaped him.

The shot, when it came, seemed as impotent as a firecracker, so Tom was surprised by the sudden revelry of the flying foxes. A distant sprout of dust marked the course the bullet had taken. Well beyond the dust, he could see the disappearing hindquarters of the dingo. It consoled him— the wide margin by which the animal had eluded the slug— and he wondered for a moment if Jim had pulled his aim.

Jim was prying the shell from the gun's stubborn breach, mumbling under his breath. He broke into an embarrassed laugh when the shell dropped finally to the ground. "The cheeky little bugger," he said. "You were right about one thing. He's lucky as sin. In Queensland he'd have been a corpse long ago."

November 18, 1978: For the People of Jonestown, Guyana
A premonition on the eve of the incident
By Ollie Mae Trost Welch

I muse along a lonely way
Among untrodden paths I stray
Obscured in sodden woods I tread
Where Winter's Autumn leaves have bled
Is this the scent that surely led
The poet to these unsung dead?

To these generations of molten leaves
The imagination is molded and fed
The fermenting mind begins to see
The very first leaf untimely shed
Then countless others, in precious colors
Pirouetting on a thread
Into time's net obscurely spread.

The hour's catch eternally wed
Rejoins earth's consummate bed
And feathered by these molten leaves
Nature's darkened wings have bred
Winter's phoenix rising from the ash
Restores Autumn's crown of gold and red.

My muse refuses to go away
It's Jonestown's tragedy I portray
Those faithful people led astray
Blasting the ghastly news all day
Their gentle innocence I do share
Their bitter, untimely fate unfair
Poetic words alone cannot repair.

Pierced Ears
By Elise Frances Miller

TO BRENDA, THE NEW GIRL looked like a kindergartener. Brenda had found herself staring at Alena ever since Mrs. Fox introduced her to the second grade class that Monday morning. Besides being too small for seven, Alena had these tiny silver jewels in her ears. They sparkled when the indoor light hit them, like glitter. Brenda couldn't take her eyes off of them. She wondered how the new girl kept them there. Had her Mama glued them on?

When it rained on Wednesday, the children filed into the auditorium for folkdance. As they entered the big, warm space, Brenda saw Alena shivering and watching the others line up. Everyone else knew the routine. As the tallest girl in the class, Brenda went to one end of the girls' line. She looked down along the faces of her friends and there was Alena, as she expected, moping at the other end. The new girl bent her head so low that her thin, sandy-colored bangs covered her eyes, and she clasped her hands tightly behind her back.

Brenda was glad they were in the cozy auditorium. She was sure that if a strong enough gust of wind came up outside, little Alena would be blown across the playground like brown autumn leaves. Theirs was a broad suburban playground, out in back of the brand new school, built for the large crops of children moving onto the San Francisco Peninsula, year after year, in the 1950s. The playground had unobtrusive plantings of dusty trees, transplanted to California, that lost all their leaves this time of year. Brenda loved to listen to the leaves crunch when she tromped on them. Sometimes they gathered in roly-poly clusters and blew over the blacktop until they settled along the chain-link fence. That's what Alena would do, Brenda decided. Then Mrs. Fox would have to go fetch her before the janitor threw her into the big garbage bin.

Brenda giggled, then paid attention to Mrs. Fox, who had finished twiddling the portable record player dials and now walked down the middle of the two rows, the fidgety boys facing the girls in their nice, straight line. When she reached the far end of the line, Mrs. Fox held out her hand to Brenda. Oh no! Brenda was sure she would have to dance with the teacher again.

But Mrs. Fox said, "Brenda, today I would like you to help me out." Holding hands, they walked slowly all the way back to the other end of the girls' line. "Alena is new, and she doesn't know our dances," Mrs. Fox said as they walked. "I would like you to be her partner and to show her the steps." Everyone listened. Even the boys stopped whispering. They sure stared though. And Bad Jack sniggered, as usual.

The teacher drew Brenda's hand toward Alena's sweaty one. Brenda grabbed it and leaned toward Alena so she could examine the silver earrings up close. They were so *very* pretty, shining under the auditorium lights. Brenda smiled at Alena, whose face remained motionless and terribly serious.

"Brenda, please take Alena over to the side," Mrs. Fox pointed, "and show her what we do, one step at a time. Please be patient."

The music came on and masked the storm outside. Brenda focused on her task. Lucky for her, Alena paid attention, following every step. Soon they moved together properly. The little girl smiled up at her.

"You're a good dancer!" Brenda giggled and shouted over the music. "Now watch the others," she instructed. "See how they take partners and go around in the circle while they dance?" Alena watched. "Do you see?"

"Yes, I see," Alena said. Her words came out firm and thick, as if she had a stuffy nose. Brenda realized that she had never heard Alena speak before. She sounded different, kind of like Grandma and Grandpa. Brenda thought that maybe Alena didn't know how to talk any better than she knew how to dance.

"Good girl." Brenda patted the little girl on the shoulder. Suddenly, Brenda realized that Alena would learn to talk as quickly as she learned to dance if they all talked to her. "Alena," she said. "Are you from America?" Alena looked at her feet. "Don't worry! It's okay. Mrs. Fox says everyone in America or their relatives started out in a different country."

"But you are not from a different country!" Alena blurted out.

"My Grandma and Grandpa are from Hungary," Brenda said proudly. "That's in Europe. They sound like you when they speak. But my Grandma doesn't have shiny earrings like you. I really like them. Can I touch?" Alena nodded. Brenda put one finger out and stroked. She expected them to be cool, but they felt warm, like Alena's ear. "Thank you," she said, remembering her manners.

"You are welcome."

"Do you know where Hungary is?" Alena nodded.

"Were you born there?" Brenda asked hopefully. Alena shook her head. "Where were you born, then?"

"In DP camp," Alena murmured.

Brenda brightened. "Oh, a camp? My mama and I went to a Brownie camp last summer for three nights. They had horses! Do you like horses?"

Alena interrupted. "No horses. I seen horses in pictures. You saw real horse?"

"And rode one, too! And brushed him! That's a funny camp you were at."

"It was DP camp in *Chess-key*." She stared at Brenda expectantly, her pale eyes opened wide. Then she said, "Ahhh! To you, *Chssslvka,* near to Hungary."

It sounded to Brenda like Alena had said a nonsense word. "Oh sorry," Brenda said. "I don't think I understand you."

"Don't mind, not important," Alena said. "Anyway, America is better."

They watched the dancers silently until the record ended. Brenda felt confused, but still curious, like she had an itch on her back that she couldn't reach. Mrs. Fox turned the record player off and came over to the two girls. "Can Alena dance now?" she asked.

"Yes, I *dance*!" Alena declared loudly. She took Brenda's hand and the little thing pulled her big partner back into the line. Brenda grinned, watching Alena's silver jewels glisten in front of her.

❖

After school that day, Brenda decided to ask Mama about Alena's earrings. As Mama swept the kitchen linoleum, Brenda followed her across the room, telling her all about the new girl Alena, who had earrings like a grownup.

"Pierced ears," Mama nodded, knowingly. "They do that to girls in other countries."

"Pierced? You mean they make a hole? Eewww!"

Mama laughed, handing Brenda the dust pan. The girl dropped to her knees and held the pan firm for her mother, who chatted on. "They say it doesn't hurt if they do it in the center of the lobe, right *there*." Mama bent down and pointed at her own smooth ear lobe. "But most American women are just as happy to use clip-ons. And it's so unnecessary to do that to a child."

They washed their hands. Mama began to cut up salad vegetables on the drain board. Brenda sat on a stool next to her mother, cutting buttered bread into little squares with the dull knife. She liked working alongside Mama at the gleaming yellow drain board. And she especially liked making the croutons. Mama's part would be to put them on a cookie sheet and bake them when she finished with her squares.

"Do you know if Alena is from another country, like Grandma and Grandpa?" Mama asked.

"Yes, but not Hungary." Brenda chuckled, "She *looks* 'hungry' though." She expected her mother to smile at the pun they had all repeated at one time or another, but Mama bent over her lettuce, chopping and frowning. Brenda continued, "She is way too small for second grade. She's short *and* skinny!"

"Well, never tease her."

"I wouldn't!"

"She probably didn't get enough vitamins as a baby," Mama said.

"Why not?"

Mama sighed and frowned again. "Because some people are not as lucky as we are."

"Mama, where is Zech-ol-ska?" Brenda pronounced it as carefully as she could remember.

"I *think* that's *Check-oo-slow-vak-ee-ah*."

"But it sounded different when Alena said it."

"Maybe she said something like *Chess-key*."

"Yes! That's it! And there's another place," Brenda continued. "Called DP. Is that in Europe, too? Alena said she was born in 'DP camp'."

Mama put down her knife and suddenly seemed a little scared, which made Brenda more curious than frightened. "What else did she say?"

Brenda shrugged. "I told her about Brownie camp but DP camp didn't have horses. And then she said the camp was in this *Chess-key* place."

Mama sighed and picked up her knife. "We'll have to talk about this after dinner. I may have a book or a map I can show you. Now finish the croutons and go play until Daddy comes home."

Brenda heard the basketball bouncing against the garage door. She finished her bread squares and ran outside to play.

"What were you and Mama talking about?" Howie asked right away, then tossed his sister the ball. She took a shot that missed. "Here," he said. He placed Brenda right in front of the basket. "Stand right here and *aim*." The ball hit the rim and fell onto the driveway. He caught it after the first bounce. "You shot better! You hit the rim."

"Do I get any points for that?"

Howie smiled and cleared his throat, trying not to laugh at her. Brenda knew her big brother liked playing with her, even though he was eleven years old. Most of the time he treated her like a friend, but she was always wary. He could also be mean sometimes, really nasty.

Howie improvised. "Depends on what kind of game you're playing. We'll make this game one point for the rim, two if it goes through the basket. Wanna play?"

He won anyway, of course. Brenda never made a basket, but she had lots of rim points. As they walked across the patio and flopped into the plastic-covered chairs to rest, Howie remembered. "What did you and Mama talk about before?" he asked again. "Before you came out to the garage? I peeked in the kitchen window and Mama looked kind of upset."

"She said that we were lucky because we had vitamins and that Alena in my class is small because she didn't," Alena replied, trying to sum it up. "She didn't feel like talking about it anymore."

"Hmmm. I don't remember Alena. Has she played over here?"

"She's new. Just came into the second grade this week."

Howie sat forward and seemed excited. "Hey, maybe we should get together a food package for her lunch."

"Naw, she's okay now. Mama said she didn't eat enough where she came from in Europe. But she eats a sandwich and apple or carrot for lunch, like I do."

Howie sat back, relaxed. Then he sighed, just like Mama. "We sure are lucky! And I think I heard Daddy! I'm starved."

"Me, too. Let's go!"

❖

Brenda understood by her mother's hesitation that talking about Alena would break their family rule: only good news at the dinner table. So after dinner, when Mama asked her to go play with Howie upstairs, she went obediently.

From the bedroom, Howie and Brenda could hear the rumbling of their parents' conversation. The tension rose in Daddy's voice almost like it did with the ballgame on TV and the San Francisco Seals at bat, but tonight they heard no cheers, and no boos either.

"Come do the puzzle," Howie said, closing the door. "You can't hear them anyway."

"But I know it's about me. And Alena, the new girl in my class. And now I'm so curious I could scream."

"Hey doofus, get used to being left out. They're not gonna tell you about it anyway."

"About what? Do you know?"

Howie cocked his head and grinned, but his lips spread too tight like for the third try at a photo smile. "Sure I do," he bragged. "I know *everything*." He sat down on the bed, with Brenda poised over him.

"Tell me, *pleeeeze*, oh please, Howie!" Brenda begged.

"Can't."

"Why not?"

"Cause they'd kill me."

Brenda groaned. "If you don't tell *I'm* gonna be the dead one."

"Then you'll be just like all of them."

"Who?"

"The Jews in Europe."

Brenda's mouth opened wide but only a tiny "ohhh" slid out. Her fists pushed against her hips. "But Alena is alive. So *you're* the doofus!"

"Leave me alone," Howie barked.

Brenda did a shout-whisper. "Tell me! Tell me now, you *meanie*!" She climbed onto the bed and started to pummel her brother. "Now! quick! Tell me now, you *meanie*," she kept repeating, the pitch of her voice escalating and tears starting to well up. Howie deflected her little fists and lifted her off the bed to the carpet.

Brenda crumpled between his legs, still beating at his calves. "Ow, stop that," Howie yelled and grabbed her wrists. "Go to hell!" Now Brenda really started to cry. Howie let loose his grip, but held her arms away.

Suddenly, his words came quick, blasting out of his mouth. He was a monster spitting fire. "You want to know?" Howie shouted down at Brenda. "Those Germans stole little Jewish children like you right out of their houses and shot them in the street and the blood ran like dirty red rainwater in the gutters."

Brenda started to laugh, a low, throaty laugh almost like a growl. "You're just trying to scare me, but you're a dirty liar."

"Every country in Europe *crawled* with boogiemen!" Howie snarled, raising his arms, elbows bent. "I'm coming to get you..." Brenda squirmed back away from him, so he dropped to his knees, his clawed fingers still poised and threatening. "The Germans *hated* the Jews. But they couldn't kill them all in the street, so they loaded them up in train cars like cows. They took them to camps and burned them all up!"

"No!" Brenda screeched, covering her ears. "You're lying. No one ever did that!"

"But there were *still* too many, so they left thousands and thousands in prisons with no food and they starved and they all looked like skeletons and there were *piles* of bones, big mountains of skeleton bones!" Howie's hands shot up above his head. His fingers quivered and he suddenly let loose a yowl with a keening wail at the end, "Hallow*eeeeen*?" Her brother's eyes were up on the ceiling, like he had forgotten she was in the room. "Halloween dead," he cried to the ceiling. "But some still *breeeathed*, so finally they covered all the people with tons of dirt so they were dead, dead, dead!"

Brenda's hands still covered her ears. She whimpered and giggled at the same time. But Howie had finally relaxed his hands and sat back. He was sweating; tears leaked from his eyes. He took in a big gulp of air and swiped at his eyes. "It's true, I swear," he whined. "The fifth graders watched a movie about it at Temple Shalom. The Nuremberg movie."

Brenda stood up, squaring her shoulders. Defiantly, she shouted at him, "You're a stupid dumb liar, that's what you are. No one ever did that to kids and regular people!

Halloween's not real. And there is no boogie man. You're just being mean, mean, mean!"

Howie kept silent as she stared him down. "Anyway," he finally said, shrugging his shoulders, "the war ended and they sent the rest of them to better camps for people without houses because the Germans took all their houses away. They're called Displaced Person camps. Initials DP. That's what you asked mom about. I heard you. And then they came to the U.S."

"You're a crazy boy," Brenda said. "I'm never going to believe another word you say, ever."

Howie blew his nose. He handed his sister a Kleenex and she did the same. She started to do the puzzle. Howie came over and gave her an edge piece. He tried to show her where it went, but she pushed his hand away.

Mama slowly opened the door. "Were you two fighting?"

"No," they both answered at once.

"Yes," Brenda reversed herself. "I wanted to do the puzzle myself and Howie bothered me."

Mama told Howie to go find Daddy and she sat on the bed. "Brenda, you know the war Daddy fought in Europe, right?" Brenda nodded. She could feel her heart beating fast.

"Well, after we won, everyone wanted to come live in America, but they couldn't all come at once. So Alena's parents had to wait their turn. They waited in a DP camp in Europe. DP means 'Dis*placed* Persons,' like people with no other *place* to be while they are waiting to get to a new home. Alena was born there, then they came here. And that's the story."

Brenda put down the puzzle piece she had been gripping so tightly between her fingers that its edges curled. She went to sit next to Mama on the bed, resting her head on Mama's stomach. Mama stroked her hair. "Why didn't she get enough vitamins?" Brenda asked.

"Because there were so many Jews it was hard to feed them all properly. They probably didn't always have enough food in the camp."

Brenda's mouth felt dry, but she wasn't thirsty or hungry either. "So many Jews" is what Howie had said, or was it "still too many Jews?" But his Jews were dead, not alive and hungry. She tried to swallow but couldn't really do it, so she tried harder and a gulping sound escaped. "Are you alright?" Mama asked.

Brenda's hand shot up to her ear. She pinched the lobe between her thumb and forefinger. "Did it hurt much when they cut her ear?" she whispered.

"Oh, darling," Mama's head bent so that their ears were side by side, "they don't cut, they pierce straight through and it doesn't hurt. I'm sure her parents did it when Alena was very young, to make her prettier. It does, doesn't it?"

"Yes, very pretty. And I like her, Mama. Will she be all right now?"

"Of course! She'll probably learn English and grow bigger in no time." Mama laughed and gave her daughter a squeeze, then stood up and stretched. Brenda sat up, feeling better, trying to absorb Mama's chirpy reminder that it was time to get ready for bed. She watched her Mama edge toward the door and disappear down the hall.

Brenda crossed to her dresser and opened the pajama drawer slowly, as if she were afraid something might jump out at her. Howie *must* have made up that boogieman story to scare her, she thought. Of course, those things could never be real! She stood for a long time with her hands resting inside the pajama drawer, sunk into the soft flannel. She was determined not to cry. She knew she would probably have nightmares. But, she told herself, even nightmares were not real.

Second Wives
By Dorcas Cheng-Tozun

WE WERE DISPLACING our landlord's mistress. Or so said our real estate agent, Nicole, a tiny woman with fashionably square glasses and an incessantly ringing mobile phone. I didn't believe her until my husband, Ned, actually met the mistress the day he signed the lease for a two-bedroom flat in Shenzhen, China.

"What's she like?" I couldn't help asking. Ned was in China, making arrangements for our upcoming move; I was still in California, closing out my job and packing.

"She's really young, maybe in her early twenties. She had a little dog in her purse."

"What does she look like?"

Ned knew me well enough to know what I was really asking. "She's not that pretty," he assured me.

"Is she skinny?"

"I guess. But she's not that attractive."

Ned's loyalty satisfied me but his minimal descriptions did not. I tried again. "What's the dog like?"

"Small. Furry. Yippy."

"What kind of dog is it?"

"I don't know." Ned began to sound irritated. "Why does it matter?"

"It doesn't," I admitted. But it was my first encounter with a mistress, and there was so much I wanted to know.

Fortunately, Nicole's frequent visits to other people's homes gave her quite a bit of insight into their lives, and she had no qualms about sharing the intimate details with us. Mr. Lim, a Hong Kong man in his sixties who inhabited a scrawny, hunched body and wore bifocals on a delicate chain around his neck, had been inspired by the housing boom just over the border in Shenzhen and had purchased this flat several years ago as an investment. He told his wife and teenage son that he would stay there whenever he did business in mainland China. But he didn't stay there alone. He was one of *those* men, Nicole told us, well-to-do men from China, Taiwan, or Hong Kong who acted like the polygamy common in Imperial China was still legal and socially acceptable. *Ernai*, the mistresses are still called. *Second wives.*

Shenzhen had been little more than a fishing village when the central government decided to build up its infrastructure and loosen regulations to encourage economic growth. By 2008, the year we moved there, Shenzhen and its surrounding areas had become one of the world's leading manufacturing regions. Most of the city's ten million residents were migrants from every corner of China, drawn by the promise of better jobs.

The relaxed government oversight, the influx of businessmen with cash, and the high numbers of young, uneducated women created the perfect conditions for a surge in illicit sexual relationships. *Ernai* became so prevalent in Shenzhen that the rail line connecting it to Hong Kong is sometimes called the Concubine Express.

It was probably right around the time we were preparing to move overseas that Mr. Lim's long-suffering wife was complaining about the Shenzhen apartment. Why should the flat sit vacant most of the time, she reasoned, when it could provide a handsome income for the family if rented out? Mr. Lim couldn't come up with a good explanation that didn't involve confessing his indiscretions, so the mistress got downgraded to a smaller, cheaper apartment to make room for new tenants. And not just tenants, but co-conspirators. Like it or not, when we signed our lease, we had become complicit in Mr. Lim's affair, providing cover for him and his clandestine activities.

We didn't know for sure where the mistress went after we commandeered her flat, though we suspected she had been moved to a part of Shenzhen nicknamed *ernai cun*, or *mistress village*. The neighborhood's defining characteristics were its disproportionately high number of single-occupancy female tenants and its frequent nighttime visitors. As soon as most shops and restaurants in the city closed at 10 p.m., taxi drivers often went to *ernai cun*, where business would surely be bustling.

For months after we moved into our apartment, the existence of Mr. Lim's mistress—even in a distant corner of the city—felt vaguely threatening to me. She represented a category of people that I would rather not be forced to acknowledge: women who were either so desperate or had such a relaxed sense of morality that they would provide sexual favors to men, regardless of their age or marital status, in exchange for a flat and some pocket money.

I would sometimes contemplate the swarming crowds around us and wonder how many women in the city were actively seeking a rich businessman to sponsor them. I already knew that Ned—with his boyish good looks, his polite mannerisms, and his obvious ambition—fit the profile of the kind of man that some Chinese women would target. When he had conducted interviews for an administrative assistant position a couple months before we moved, nearly every candidate he interviewed had tried to flirt her way into being hired. They giggled, blushed, and batted their eyelashes in response to his questions. Some went so far as to interrupt the interview to ask if he was married or tell him how handsome he was. Wise man that he is, Ned ended up hiring a woman who was older than us and happily married.

To make myself feel better, I would sometimes walk a little bit closer to Ned when we were out on the streets of Shenzhen. When I did, I often caught Chinese Nationals staring at us, and even more intentionally looking away from us. I was sure it was because of Ned's otherness—his height, his lighter coloring, his language.

Only much later did I realize it was because of me.

It didn't take us long to understand that the *ernai*, with their rent-free apartments and plush monthly allowances, are actually at the top of an extensive sex hierarchy in Shenzhen. Far below them are the women whose services are peddled by pimps on the city's sidewalks, offered as casually as if they were proffering counterfeit DVDs or handbags, as well as the women who work in "spas" that provide much more than the typical massage. And then there are the Chinese women who are neither *ernai* nor prostitutes, but who specifically target foreign men in hopes of a better life or a passport out of the country.

These were the women who had fawned over Ned and fluttered their eyelashes when he interviewed them. These were the women who smiled at him like he was a gift from heaven whenever he entered a store or restaurant.

As a wife who had every intention of keeping her husband to herself, I couldn't help but feel annoyed, even angry, with these Chinese women. But I knew that many of the foreign men in Shenzhen—primarily European and American businessmen—were just as much to blame. They readily encouraged the flirtations of Chinese women, their heads swelling to the point of bursting whenever beautiful Chinese girls hung on their arms like dinner towels.

We regularly saw these couples strolling around the city. We sometimes overheard their stilted interactions when we went out to eat, the woman usually professing her devotion in broken English and the man dismissing her as little more than his post-meal entertainment.

I stewed over how wrong it all was. But as I noticed more and more people on the streets who refused to meet my gaze, a disturbing thought came to me.

"What do you think people think about me when they see us together?" I asked Ned.

He and I both watched as a plump middle-aged Caucasian man who looked like a cross between Chris Farley and Donald Trump, accompanied by a slender Chinese woman with wide eyes and a beautiful smile, passed us.

"I'm sure people can tell you're an American," he assured me.

I wasn't convinced. "I don't think people know I'm not from here."

"But you look so different from everyone else." He gestured toward my petite frame, black hair, and dark eyes as if they screamed anything but *Chinese*.

I wanted to believe Ned, but I had a hard time doing so. I had begun to suspect that Shenzhen's residents, most of whom had migrated from rural areas, couldn't understand how someone ethnically Chinese could come from a place other than China. And if they assumed I was a local girl, they would naturally have to explain why I was always in the company of a tall white man.

❖

One night, Ned and I were heading home from work when two Chinese men who looked about university-aged approached us. They eyed Ned with unnaturally large grins on their faces. "Hello. We are study English in school," one of them explained. "We need practice. It's okay?"

"Where you from?" the other one interjected.

"The United States," Ned replied.

"*Wah*, United States," they exclaimed, and proceeded to ask Ned several more questions about why he was in China and how long he was planning to stay.

Eventually, one of them turned to me and began speaking in rapid Mandarin. I didn't understand his words, but I certainly understood his expression as he leisurely examined me from head to toe. Then he held up both of his hands and moved them in the shape of an hourglass. *Nice curves.*

I could feel my face flaming as I stared at him, frozen with surprise. Never before had a stranger commented on my modest B-cups and almost nonexistent hips. But to have a Chinese man do this, in a culture where sex and sexuality are never mentioned in polite company, was shocking.

I wanted to say something biting in return, to casually toss back a retort that would shame him for his inappropriate behavior. But my Mandarin was so poor that I literally had no words.

"What did they say?" Ned asked as they walked away.

I remained quiet for a few seconds before responding. "I think they think I'm a prostitute or your mistress."

"What?" he said disbelievingly. "You look nothing like a prostitute."

I appreciated his outrage, but I could only shake my head in reply.

Ned gave my arm a reassuring squeeze. "Don't worry. They're just a couple of dumb guys. They don't know anything."

But I couldn't forget the looks in those men's eyes, especially when I saw those same looks only a few weeks later. We had decided to explore one of the local markets. With both the temperature and the humidity pushing the bounds of human limits, I had worn a tank top and shorts. The shorts were not a problem, I knew, as women in Shenzhen often wore extremely short shorts, even to work. I had not noticed many tank tops, but I didn't think the V-neck on my top was particularly revealing or noticeable. But then I started to notice the pointed gazes of dozens of men around us. Some of the looks were disapproving, others were angry, and some were just transparent enough to make me feel sick.

I turned to Ned with sudden urgency. "I need to buy another shirt. I need to cover up more."

He put his arm around me and guided me into the nearest shop. Ten minutes later I emerged, wearing a new sweater like a shield against the eyes that saw only what they wanted to see.

It took just eighteen months for Shenzhen and its complex social-sexual dynamics to overwhelm me. The Chinese Nationals who didn't assume I was chasing a passport treated me like I was Ned's personal assistant or interpreter. After all, as far as they knew, that's all I could be. The messaging was so consistent that I almost believed it myself—which was when I knew I had to leave.

Ned had patiently listened to my complaints for months, had seen how the treatment I received wore my spirit down to splinters. But he refused to capitulate, stubbornly holding my hand or putting his arm around me in public, regardless of what those around us might think. Behind the scenes, he laid the groundwork for our escape, making arrangements with his company for us to move to Hong Kong. It was just a train ride away, but with its successful fusion of east and west, Hong Kong might as well have been another planet.

A couple days after we moved out, I returned to Shenzhen to pack up the last of our belongings and finish cleaning our flat. I had been cleaning for several hours when I saw a young woman standing in our open doorway. Her hair was in a fashionable bob cut, her slim figure adorned with a white ruffled blouse, a denim skirt, and a designer handbag—probably a knock-off—over one shoulder.

"*Ni hao,*" I said cautiously, swiping stray hairs out of my eyes. I was uncomfortably aware of how unkempt I must have looked in comparison to her sleek appearance, sweat and dust caking every inch of my skin.

"*Ni hao.*" She gave me a hard look. "*Ni shi shei?*" Who are you?

"I'm Ms. Cheng," I replied. When she didn't say anything, I asked, "Who are you?"

Her only acknowledgement of my question was to step over the threshold. She was halfway across the living room before she paused. "I own this place," she said, settling onto the gray and white sectional sofa that sat in the middle of the flat. She leaned back against the cushions, crossing her legs as she took a makeup compact out of her bag and began checking her reflection in the mirror. She didn't say anything more even as I stood before her, gaping at her audacity.

Finally, I knew who she was: Mr. Lim's mistress, back to reclaim her territory. But I still had an apartment to clean. For the next hour, I packed and dusted under her watchful eyes—all the while resisting the urge to flee and leave the apartment in its unfinished state, happy to sacrifice my cleaning supplies to escape the unsettling atmosphere. I could not stop thinking about how this young woman, who looked so fresh and innocent, was providing sexual favors to a man three times her age in exchange for an apartment and a comfortable lifestyle. I had to wonder why she had chosen to be an *ernai* instead of pursuing another, more reputable line of work.

But what did I really know? That was one valuable lesson that living in Shenzhen had taught me: it is never wise to make assumptions about who someone is. Perhaps this woman had chosen to be an *ernai* as much as I had chosen to be perceived as a foreign-man-hunting hussy. What I did know was that we had both been treated like dust that most people would prefer to sweep under the rug—she much more than I, no doubt.

There was, however, one key difference between us. I was empowered to leave this apartment and never look back. I could leave Shenzhen and the awful ways in which women were treated here, and move to a place where I knew I would be allowed greater dignity and respect. With Mr. Lim holding her purse strings and the Chinese government restricting her travel, this woman couldn't.

As I finished and got ready to leave, she looked up at me. I realized then that I didn't even know her name. I looked back at her, unsure what the protocol was for handing an apartment over to your landlord's mistress. After a few moments, I placed the keys on the dining room table. I wondered if I was supposed to thank her, or wish her well, but nothing sounded right in my head. So I just said, "*Zai jien*"—literally, *see you again*—and closed the door gently behind me.

The Odor Odyssey
By Bardi Rosman Koodrin

"GOD, IT STINKS IN HERE!" I stepped over two bodyboards and squeezed around a hundred-pound bench press to reach my fifteen-year-old son. Peter was lying on his bed, his nose buried in a surfing magazine instead of a textbook.

"Huh? What?" He rolled over freshly washed shirts. "My room always smells like this."

"Something died," I said. "Find it."

"Sure, okay," he said.

"I mean now."

"Ah, Ma-aa!"

My only child and I have had a number of "Ah, Ma-aa!" moments. When Peter was much younger, say the first eight-and-three-quarter months of his life, he was a sweet baby, malleable to all of my suggestions. Then, the day he turned nine months old, he got up and walked around his bedroom for the very first time. One week later, watching a gleeful baby running up and down our hallway at full speed, I knew I was in for it.

Peter negotiated my requests, demands, and threats with the skill of a diplomat. His night-light was a world globe, illuminating a microcosm of racing cars underfoot and Superman posters taped on the walls. The room smelled of trees, dirt, and little boy sweat.

One day he traded his best baseball cards for a four-foot gopher snake. It came with an aquarium and bulky leather gloves in case we needed to handle it. I took Peter to the pet store and we bought a mouse for the nasty hisser.

I'd already given him the speech. "If you want a snake, you have to feed it live prey. Are you sure you can handle this?"

"Oh sure, no problem." He nodded, convincing me with his deep brown eyes. Once we returned home, however,

Peter couldn't handle anything, even while wearing thick gloves three sizes too large.

I had to shove the bright-eyed, pink-nosed mouse to its fate. We watched in horror as the snake teased it. I tried to rescue the poor little rodent but the territorial snake kept me at bay. When Peter's dad came home, he donned the gloves and saved the fuzzy gray mouse we'd named Hunca Munca. Father and son relocated the snake to a gopher-rich habitat too far away for it to slither back.

The odors in that bedroom changed from sandboxes to sandy wet suits, bubblegum wrappers to Taco Bell bags. All through high school, Peter's room stank of his baseball player's uniform and chewing tobacco spittle. His buddies seemed right at home, and, to my surprise, the girls in their group tossed aside wet towels and magazines to sit demurely on the cleanest edge of his unmade bed.

When Peter went away to college to study the planet's more exotic locales, he left in a frenzied rush, swearing with all good intentions he'd make the room spiffy his first weekend home. When he went away to a different college the next time, I shut the door, since San Diego was too far for me to hold my breath.

In time, Peter got a job and his own place. I packed up the last of his mess.

Our niece Jill asked to stay for a month and ended up living in that room for two years. It smelled great. Peter returned, but he had to wait in the wings, in a den barely bigger than a closet. His stinky stuff spread like damp mold down the hallway, inching toward his old room. Cousin Jill soon left. Eventually Peter did too.

To save money for a grand world adventure, Peter moved home again. He was wise to stifle any leftover replies of "Ah, Ma-aa!"

While he planned his trip, I'd stand on his bed in front of huge maps taped on the walls, helping him to stick red- and yellow-colored pins next to odd-sounding places he just had to visit, like Kathmandu and Karangetang.

After we bid him bon voyage, he sent emails from Internet cafes in the most remote areas of the world. I'd stand on his bed, muttering to the maps, "Oh, he's here today."

Now he's coming back home.

After roaming through Fiji, New Zealand, Australia, Bali, Sulawesi, Nepal, and Paris, Peter's heading straight for his room and fresh sheets. He'll be bearded and grungy. He'll dump his backpack, tent, and five months' worth of adventures in his bedroom. His gear will bear the scent tales of steamy jungles, where he photographed endangered horn bull birds, tiny tarsier monkeys, and even roasted dogs and bats for sale in Cambodian open markets.

I wonder what having slept in grass huts on tropical islands and on ice while camping on a glacier with penguins will smell like? He probably won't be able to help bringing home the aromas from his thirty-two-hour bus ride from Singapore to Bangkok and the cremation ceremony he witnessed beside the Bagmati River in Kathmandu.

I can hardly wait to say, "God, it stinks in here!"

Just You and Me
A pantoum
By Jo Carpignano

You are like the wind
Combing grasses on the hill
I am like the sea
Confined from shore to shore

Combing grasses on the hill
I envy you your freedom
Confined from shore to shore
Yearning to fly free as you

I envy you your freedom
Sweeping snow from alpine slopes
Yearning to fly free as you
Echoing between the canyon walls

Sweeping snow from alpine slopes
I listen to your symphony of sound
Echoing between the canyon walls
I cannot follow, shores forbid my wandering

I listen to your symphony of sound
While roaring my objection to outrageous ties
I cannot follow, shores forbid my wandering
Helplessly I batter the restrictive rock

While roaring my objection to outrageous ties
You hear my voice and come to join my storm
Helplessly I batter the restrictive rock
And when we come together, energy explodes

You hear my voice and come to join my storm
I gather strength from your embrace
And when we come together, energy explodes
Your echoes amplified within my roar

I gather strength from your embrace
We come together in orgasmic explosions
Your echoes amplified within my roar
The earth trembles under forces of our intercourse

Fruit Fly in the Chardonnay
By Linda Okerlund

IT WAS A HOT AFTERNOON in late August. Indian Summer, although given the current population of Silicon Valley, the term brings to mind images of New Delhi and curried meats rather than Native American tribes roasting turkey and ears of corn with the pilgrims.

I sat in the shade of my porch reading some 1960-ish beat poet or another, sipping wine, and pondering writings that now seemed utterly banal given modern societal norms. "We're all golden sunflowers inside" and "Follow your inner moonlight; don't hide the madness." How times have changed.

I swirled my glass and took another sip, preparing to savor the sweetness of late summer. Looking down into the glass, I spotted a small black speck. Looking closer, I saw it had wings. From the long-forgotten genetic experiments performed in high school to demonstrate concepts of Mendelian genetics, I could identify it as *Drosophila melanogaster*. A fruit fly.

Upon my family's arrival here in 1969, this area was known as the Santa Clara Valley, and was still largely agricultural. Apricots. Almonds. Walnuts. Prunes. The house we moved into had a tree-filled yard that was, by my six-year-old standards, enormous. Lemons. Limes. Apricots. Peaches. Figs. I never tasted the figs. In fact, I never tasted figs at all outside of the Newton until my mid-thirties. Yet I hated that tree for the fact that I was the one responsible for cleaning the mess in the yard when the over-ripe fruit fell to the ground.

There were lots of kids in the neighborhood, and I was friends with three or four of them. On long summer afternoons we would ride our bikes to the end of the block and into a medium-sized apricot orchard. The area appeared deserted. Tumbleweeds blew down the street. We amused ourselves by riding aimlessly through the orchard, occasionally pelting one another with squishy fruit that had fallen to the ground but hadn't yet attracted flies. We would pick softened apricots, biting into them and letting the sweet juice run down our chins and onto our shirts. We felt safe but adventurous, having to protect ourselves only from an occasional stray golf ball from the adjacent range. Sometimes we'd collect the balls and present them proudly to neighborhood fathers.

Over the years, as I moved from elementary, to middle, and finally to high school, I saw the landscape change, imperceptibly at first, or perhaps merely in ways I failed to notice. One at a time, the orchards were plowed under in favor of the silicon chip.

Attending high school in the late seventies, I knew several families who had been persuaded to sell their orchards to real estate developers. In one case, the state imposed its power of eminent domain to purchase the middle section of a prune orchard to build a road. This conveniently linked parts of town, but split the farm in half. The family sold the more distant half. Cultivating the remaining land became increasingly difficult as new housing developments were planted around it. The land grew more valuable, less due to its yield than to its location. Finally, the temptation became too great.

Dot-com style wealth began to bloom in this agrarian society, many years prior to the computer era that the farmers unwittingly fertilized with the sale of their lands. Yet this particular incarnation of the *nouveau-riche* maintained their farm ethos, living in houses no bigger than the families needed. Some even replaced their Santa Clara Valley land with acreage further north, adding boats and RVs they could use to enjoy themselves through their impending retirement once my contemporaries had graduated from high school, moving out and moving on.

Seeing the fruit fly in my wine that afternoon unleashed a flood of memories. Even as the orchards were slowly being sold off, the mere sighting of a fruit fly was enough to generate county-wide alerts, prohibiting fruit from moving either into or out of the county. As the infestations grew more serious, the quarantined areas grew larger, presenting a true threat to the local economy. Weekly broadcasts reported the exact number of flies trapped, emphasizing the number of fertile females caught. At one point, it was decided that a reasonable means to limit the growing population would be to release a large number of sterile females. But because a significant fraction of the released females were not, in fact, sterile, the population continued to grow.

As a last resort, helicopters were dispatched to spray malathion, deadly to the flies but thought safe to humans. The helicopters disseminated clouds of the poison weekly to each region within the county. This being California, the citizenry's biggest concern was the potential effects on their cars and their paint jobs. Of secondary concern was the potential effect on the population. The government reassured everyone that there were no known effects upon automotive pigments, yet people were encouraged to wash their cars the morning after a spraying in their area. There were no known effects on people, although all were advised to remain indoors during spraying.

The spraying, which happened several times during my tenure at one of the many run-of-the-mill South Bay high schools, would continue for months at a time, always under the cover of night. No one thought much about this; we went on with our lives. As adolescents, we thought ourselves invincible and I don't recall any of our parents suggesting that we be especially careful.

Our area was scheduled for spraying on one particular Friday. That evening I attended a school dance with my boyfriend of the moment. He was a football player. I was a cheerleader. After the dance, we decided to head out for pizza and other teen festivities with a group of friends, predominantly other football players and their cheerleader girlfriends.

The two of us raced his VW bug crazily behind a yellow Chevy mini-truck toward the nearest pizza parlor. Several large pizzas and pitchers of Coke later, we were once again looking for something to do. We proceeded to the house owned by the parents of the yellow Chevy truck driver, located down a dirt road immediately off of the same connector road that several years previously had divided another family's farm and precipitated its sale. Nevertheless, the remaining homes were surrounded by fruit trees and provided a great place to party. Silent and hidden.

We emerged from our caravan of three cars and the truck to the noise of multiple helicopters overhead. The movies *Full Metal Jacket* and *Apocalypse Now* were fresh in our minds as we imagined ourselves in our own little battle scene, albeit lacking any true element of danger. We reveled in the sound and the lights. We had heard that the stuff they were spraying might be harmful, but we didn't care. We looked up at the sky to feel the spray on our faces and arms. Minutes later, the noise and commotion subsided and the droplets settled on the foliage.

That house no longer exists. Years later, the state acquired the street and its houses by eminent domain and replaced them with the last freeway to be built in the Bay Area.

And here I was, some twenty-five years later and twenty-five miles north, sitting on my porch drinking wine. Contemplating a little bug that had caused such a panic. Twenty-five years later, I still recall vividly the weekly descent of the helicopters and my frequent drives home from college 200 miles south. Two or three times along the way, a highway patrolman would stop and question me about whether I was transporting fruit.

"No officer, I only have dirty laundry and a half-finished term paper."

Now, the area is known as Silicon Valley. Apple is no longer a fruit; a web no longer requires a spider, but a cache of servers. Cash crops are silicon chips, rather than dried apricots. Levees have been erected to keep out the bay, which in earlier centuries routinely flooded to generate the valley's fertile soil, which first made it famous. The fertility of the soil matters less now that the most valuable earth has been paved. Homes have been built over the wetlands, which are no longer wet, and the foothills carved up for still more. And that little golf course next to the orchard has been replaced by a "fabless supplier of programmable logic devices."

I dipped my finger into the wine to pick out the offending insect, flicking it off into the bushes. An eternity ago, something so innocent would have created a furor over the economic sustainability of the valley. But the silicon chip and its offspring, including software, databases, video games, internet service providers and web engines, have become our sugar daddies. I, too, make my living employed by one of these new businesses.

I still long for simpler days. Playtime in the orchard. Long drives up the Peninsula through boggy wetlands now covered in high-end houses, condos, and the businesses that drive the economic engine of Silicon Valley. I miss the affordable housing. The small bungalows, set back from the road behind a veil of trees. The real people, unconcerned with the value of their portfolios or their housing.

I never thought I'd be one to say it, but I do long for days long past.

Color Times
By Bardi Rosman Koodrin

TWO TEN-YEAR-OLD GIRLS met each week in front of Community Baptist Church. They'd been best Sunday-morning friends since they could walk and talk. On this day, Emmy Ketchum got there first. Gert showed up late, as always, bursting to show off her new red shoes but needing to pee right quick, as usual.

Running to the basement bathroom before services began, the girls passed a man they didn't know. He wore a green shirt that caught Emmy's attention. *Forest green*, she determined. If he was looking for the men's room, he was on the wrong floor. He turned the corner in a rush. *Too late to tell him now.*

"We gotta hurry and get a good seat," exclaimed Emmy. "I been looking forward to Sister Geneva Clay for weeks." The buxom woman with stick legs reminded Emmy of a red-breasted robin in her choir robe. Sister was famous in the county for belting out soulful gospels. Fussing with her hair that was braided into rows, Emmy caught a glimpse of her friend in the mirror. Gert was six days older, two inches taller, and way darker. She was colored the same as a solid chunk of coal. Emmy had begun noticing such differences in art class at school, how colors and values change, how hues blend from black to white and all the in-betweens.

She figured primary colors, those bold reds and blues, were bosses who gloried in their authority. Yellows kept to themselves. When primaries mixed together, greens, purples, and oranges showed up as secondaries, which were like good servants not talking out of place. The third group—Emmy couldn't recall its name—had no place in her box of Crayolas. Yet she saw with her own hazel eyes that a pretty pink color was born from the leader red: dripping like rain, pale to white.

Emmy had some way-back Creole running through her, tinting her outsides caramel.

About a month earlier, some of Mama's friends had told Emmy she could pass. They said she had "scandal in her blood," whatever that meant. Emmy explained to them, in a real polite manner of course, that she was happy being the way she was.

"Don't you be talking like that," Mama had scolded her when they got to themselves. "Times's still bad no matter how they say otherwise. You do what you can get."

"But Mama," Emmy protested like she always did. "President Kennedy says bad times are over. It's the '60s now and we're all equals."

"This far down South?" Mama had snorted. "You tell Mr. John to come down here on one of his freedom buses. He needs to see for himself what's going on. Those bombings and all."

"Bombings? Whatcha talking about, Mama?"

"Never you mind." Mama had given Emmy a little swat on her backside. "Pay attention. Keep your eyes straight. Watch out for what others are doing."

Emmy's eyes crossed when Mama tapped Emmy's forehead, above her nose.

"Don't you ever stop seeing, Emmy Ketchum!"

Thinking back to what Mama had really been talking about got Emmy lost inside herself.

"Let's move." Gert was so jittery she stamped her new red shoes. "We're late."

Emmy wanted to go upstairs but something was bothering her. She couldn't say for sure what it was. A feeling. *A feeling of something bad.*

So she said, "Come outside with me first." What surprised Emmy was the way she was talking—like a scaredy cat taking fright over a mouse.

"C'mon!" Emmy was feeling a strong urge to walk out of that church. Her voice got louder, squeakier. "Gert Williams. Can't you come on out just for two minutes? Please!"

Gert put on her stubborn look. "No way," she snapped.

Emmy's legs were practically running away with her. "Please. Just do it!"

Gert shook her head.

"All right," sighed Emmy. "Save me a seat. I gotta do something first."

Emmy needed to get outside, stand tall in the grass, and breathe deep. She needed to move rightaways fast. She didn't argue with herself. She simply followed the urge, the message inside her head that didn't talk with words. The message that cramped up her tummy and twisted her throat into a tight knot.

When she stepped outdoors, the air was a summer hot that was standing still, not blowing a leaf. Even the birds went quiet. She felt silly standing alone when everyone was inside singing and praising. Sister Geneva Clay was due to perform any minute.

Emmy headed back, trying to think up a good excuse for Mama.

That's when the ground started shaking. Next, she heard a blast so thunderous her hands flew up to cover her ears.

"Airplane musta crashed in a field," she mumbled.

The whitewashed church exploded in a coward's rage of red, yellow, and orange fireballs. It splintered into thousands of shards as if it were a balsa wood playhouse spilling out toy furniture and stock-still dolls. The brown brick pathway generations of churchgoers had walked upon burst apart.

Emmy looked up as towers of black smoke spiraled in the sky like haunted question marks. Mama had mentioned bombings. *Is that what just happened?* Mama said to watch out for what others are doing. *That man in the green shirt.* Emmy realized she'd never seen him before. Had he—?

Survivors stumbled about the smoldering rubble, calling out friends' names, sobbing at the silences. Emmy joined them, not knowing what else to do. Poking around the bloodstained ground, she spotted a red shoe. It was strapped to a leg the color of a chunk of coal.

The ten-year-old would keep her eyes straight forever more. She learned to recognize the colors of hatred and of love. She took note of blending hues, of what goes on in between.

After that day, she never stopped looking.

Emmy Ketchum never stopped seeing.

The Yellow Bus
A villanelle
By Jo Carpignano

She rides the yellow bus each week
Goes off to school, comes home again
She hears and sees but cannot speak

The driver is a cunning sneak
Assumes a friendly caring pose
She rides the yellow bus each week

From school one day at traffic's peak
She is the last to leave the bus
She hears and sees but cannot speak

He stops on some deserted street
Then hurriedly subdues and thrusts
She rides the yellow bus each week

Her pushing, thrashing, much too weak
Mouth opens wide in voiceless scream
She hears and sees but cannot speak

Comes home late, dress slightly torn
Her mother wonders why so worn
She rides the yellow bus each week
She hears and sees but cannot speak

Skin Deep?
By Diane Jacobson

HUNKY. GORGEOUS. STEAMY. PERFECT.
These were some of the words the regulars at the 3rd Street Starbucks used to describe their barista. But none of these words quite captured his magnificence. Eddy, beautiful Eddy, worked the weekday morning shift behind the espresso machine. A rotating schedule of employees grew immune to his charms over time as they took orders for skinny sugar-free vanilla lattes and tall Americanos. They transcribed each order in a column of codes and checkmarks on disposable cups before passing them to Eddy.

Eddy methodically steamed milk, ground beans, and pumped flavorings. Never rushing, never quite dawdling. No matter how long the line or how many cups he had to fill, he moved at the same steady pace. Few patrons minded the wait for their morning jolt. If anything, they wanted him to slow down, to bestow upon them an extra moment of anticipation. Maybe, just maybe, he'd acknowledge them, share a bit of his beauty through a small smile, a nod, or even a glance. It never came.

Eddy kept his eyes on his work, despite the stream of fans. As he slipped cardboard sleeves on hot drinks and plastic straws into cold ones, he'd announce recipients and contents in a quiet, steady voice.

"Nick. Drip. Extra room. Ellen. Mocha no whip. Dustin. Caramel macchiato. Clare. Chai soy latte," he'd say, turning to the next empty cup in line.

"Thanks!" Nick and Ellen and Dustin and Clare would say. The beautiful barista never responded.

People of all ages, genders, and walks of life feasted on him, devouring him with their eyes and inserting him into their fantasies. Grandmothers, waiters, teachers, unemployed actuaries, database administrators, artists, and teenagers all felt their hearts beat a little harder and a little higher in their chests as they watched Eddy work. He lingered with them long after they left, long after their coffee drinks had passed through their bodies. He'd resurface in their sleep, behind their closed eyes during love making, or as their minds wandered to pass a slow moment. One woman saw his face when she emerged from anesthesia after oral surgery. One young man, his mind meandering around Eddy, was violently brought back to El Camino Real and a newly red light by the sharp slam of his car into a minivan.

People gawked and giggled and pulled out all the stops to catch Eddy's attention. But he kept his blond, sun-kissed head bent to his work. Female and male, straight and gay, patrons coveted his skin, stretched smooth over his strong jaw and straight, even nose. His form was just right. Lean, but not so lean that his tendons showed. Muscular, but not so muscular that he looked lumpy and tight. Eddy was just right. Maybe he was shaped through triathlons or hours catching waves on a surfboard? Maybe he played soccer and was a sculptor? Maybe he worked construction in the afternoons and ate only organic food? Whatever kind of perfect he was in each person's mind, he inspired the same internal flutters. He made them want to shed their navy suits and sales call schedules to jog along the bay, or throw down their pithy T-shirts, ill-fitting jeans, and start-up stresses to plant heirloom tomatoes. He aroused travel plans and shopping sprees. He inspired both brooding and optimism. Eddy's splendor moved people.

What these customers didn't know, what they couldn't see beyond Eddy's beauty, was that he *was* paying close attention. He knew most of the regulars well. He knew their names and drinks, of course, but he also knew about *them*. He collected fragments of their conversations and behaviors between steamer blasts.

He immediately noticed when one longtime regular, Peter, suddenly changed his standard order. Eddy knew the change was financially based. Peter used to be a cappuccino man until he was downsized. Now he ordered drip coffee. Eddy saw Peter lace the drab drink with half-and-half and sugar at the condiment station in an attempt to mimic the creamy concoction of days gone by. Once, Peter brought in

147

two little kids. Eddy knew these kids were deeply loved from the way Peter rested his hands on their shoulders and knelt to look into their eyes as they spoke. Eddy overheard one of Peter's phone conversations and discovered he was on the verge of losing his house. He could hear the tremor of desperation in Peter's voice as he ordered his coffee that day, so Eddy whipped up a cappuccino and served it as drip. When Peter discovered the mistake, he looked toward Eddy, who felt the stare from beneath a lock of his hair despite being hard at work on the next drink. Eddy smiled inside. He couldn't conjure up a job or house payment for Peter, but maybe one nice turn of luck would bring about another, and another.

Peter wasn't the only one on the receiving end of Eddy's gifts. He followed another regular, Kendra, as she navigated the online dating scene and dissected date after date with various friends as they waited in line. Eddy cringed and grew angry as Kendra's mating adventures unfolded, which ended with one jerk after another stealing a little of her buoyancy and chipping away at her hope. Eddy would slip her an extra pump of syrup or tinker with her caffeine when she seemed unusually agitated or groggy. But she deserved more. He waited and listened.

One rainy day, it all fell into place. Michael, a sweet, slightly overweight guy who always left his tips in bills, ended up in line in front of Kendra. Eddy made their drinks in tandem. "Kendra," he announced, and placed Michael's drink on one end of the bar. "Michael," he said, and placed Kendra's drink on the other end.

Kendra figured it out first and headed to the bar for Eddy's assistance in working out the mix up. Eddy saw her coming and disappeared into the storeroom on a fictional restocking errand, leaving them to sort it out themselves. The next day he saw Kendra and Michael smile at each other. On the third day, they chatted in line and, on the fourth, they lingered at the door. Eddy followed their relationship and let out a silent whoop one morning when they came in together holding hands. A few months later, he switched Kendra to decaf when she complained of nausea two days in a row. Eddy knew even before the expectant mother when it was time to start eating for two.

Eddy was always listening closely and remembering. Customers willingly shared their coffee preferences and their first names, which Eddy committed to memory. He paired this information with their snippets of conversation and tucked it all away in a tidy mental database. Over time he learned last names, places of employment, and vacation destinations. Insider information on city hall activities, gossip and scuttlebutt, and hush-hush IPO news trickled in. He observed his customers' personalities and interactions and tucked the data away for a rainy day.

He'd been making half-decaf, half-Splenda, extra-foam lattes for a hot number named Heather for almost a year. She clearly took good care of herself and always dressed in snug exercise clothing that artfully displayed her hard-earned smooth skin and cleavage. Heather frequently held court, ripping apart anyone who wasn't present. "God, what is she thinking getting those tacky extensions?" she'd ask a companion and move on to her next victim without waiting for an answer. "It's just shameful what that little girl wears. I'm sorry, I don't care if you are five years old, leggings are not pants. What does that say about her parents? Vulgar. Slutty. I just don't think I can let my Emma spend time over there anymore."

Eddy slowly altered Heather's drink over the period of a few weeks until he was treating the bitch to full-fat, full-sugar lattes. Then he started watching for dimples to appear through her spandex. His handiwork became visible on days she dressed in white or pale pink, but only to someone looking closely. He knew she saw it every time she got dressed. He could envision her twisting around, frowning at her ass in front of a full-length mirror. The vision filled him with warmth, as though he'd stepped from an air-conditioned building into the sunshine.

Heather wasn't the only coffee drinker who landed on Eddy's shit list. Frank, a jerk with a penchant for massive iced mochas and droopy pants, rubbed him the wrong way even before he set foot in Starbucks. One morning a high-pitched bark drew Eddy's attention to the window. He couldn't see the dog but he saw Frank pull open the door with a mobile phone pressed to his ear. "Sorry, dude what were you saying? I lost you for a second when a fricking yap dog got under my foot."

Eddy stiffed him on the chocolate and gave him decaf that first day, hoping never to see the guy again. But Frank became a regular. A regular asshole. He took cuts by ordering over the pastry case. Whenever he was in line behind an attractive female he'd close the gap until he was almost pressed against her back. Age didn't matter. Eddy had seen him brush up against a girl still wearing a training bra. Frank crumpled napkins, shot garbage-bin baskets, and left every missed shot on the floor. He clogged the unisex bathroom toilet on more than one occasion. And not once, not one single time, did Eddy see an admiring look from Frank coming his way.

Unfortunately for Frank, his job as a gas line inspector required a large lanyard and badge that Eddy noted and remembered. Also unfortunately for Frank, Eddy managed to get his hands on some methamphetamine. Eddy knew exactly which iced mocha would be Frank's last for five-to-ten. Years.

An anonymous tip about a meth-head inspector brought all hell down on Frank, whose spotty performance reviews encouraged his employer to follow up the call with a random drug test. The test came out positive and Frank was turned over to local law enforcement. When Eddy heard a couple of customers chatting about how scary it was that a meth addict had been inspecting the major gas pipes running through town, he couldn't help but crack a tiny smile.

Yes, the beautiful barista was listening.

Private Altar
By Karen Hartley

The rack was white
Its wrought iron caught
the late afternoon sunlight
and cast its shadow against the old
adobe wall
The rack held an arrangement
of flowers
for all to see
standing tall and regal

A gold filigree cross
nestled in the center of roses
and white flowers
It must have taken hours
to compose
the private altar

He came each day
to do his work
Shining shoes and sharing news
with customers young and old

I watched and waited
a long while to see
if anyone noticed his
private altar
but me
No one did

They all walked away
in their newly polished shoes
Never giving a thought to
inquiring about
his holy Muse

His day done, he
packed his caddy
and neatly placed the saddle soap
the shoe horn, cloth, polish
and brush

Then he set the caddy down
so he could touch
that cross ever so gently

I came back several times
to that place
But never saw the
shoeshine man's face
A few paces away
I could only see him do his work
and hear his pleasant voice
Only watch him quietly
finish his day, then stand again
in front of his
private altar
and say
what could only be
thanks

It's rare to see such things
today
And I felt blessed to observe
that display

The next time I went to the
old adobe building
I found they both
had gone

The shoeshine man
and his
private altar
had moved on

Lose the Bubble, Screw the Pooch, Buy the Farm
By Kevin Arnold

THE U.S. MILITARY IS FAMOUS for its jargon. In training to fly jets off aircraft carriers, there are three phrases for having messed up: *lost the bubble, screwed the pooch,* and *bought the farm.*

"Lost the bubble" means the pilot received more input than he could process. In the classroom or in a flight simulator it's embarrassing, but the stakes increase with altitude.

"Screwed the pooch" refers to a sin of commission. If a pilot stayed out late and overslept so long that his superiors canceled his hop or if he flunked a test in ground school, he'd screwed the pooch. If he made a pass at a woman in the officer's club and later learned she was an instructor's wife, he'd *definitely* screwed the pooch.

"Bought the farm" is a euphemism for crashed and died. Rumor has it that the phrase sprang from a government death benefit that paid off the family farm. Crashing and dying wasn't all that uncommon. One visiting commander casually revealed that "on a peacetime cruise, we expect to lose fifteen percent of our carrier planes and ten percent of our pilots."

Art Anthony couldn't get that statistic out of his head.

Unlike in *Catch* 22, Navy pilots in Art's day were volunteers. The procedure to leave was called Dropped on Own Request, shortened to the acronym DOR. Thoughts of DORing haunted Art, and not just for his personal survival. He wasn't sure he could push that red button he'd seen in training films—the one to the left of the stick that would drop a bomb on people he didn't know. And if he did manage to steel himself up for the task, he wasn't sure he could live with himself afterwards.

Art was a good pilot when he was focused. But he had been known to lose the bubble. He wasn't afraid of flying, but was starting to wonder if being a Navy pilot, as much as he enjoyed being aloft, was for him.

❖

Aloft on a training hop in his fifth month at Pensacola, Art saw something he didn't understand. Through the phones, he asked his instructor, "Is that smoke down there?"

"Those dots are crash trucks. I'll take over." The instructor flew down low where they could more clearly see a plane nose-down on the runway. A wisp of grey smoke rose from the plane. "I'll take us back."

The trainees were assembled and informed that the student pilot had improperly trimmed his flaps. "Shortly after takeoff, the plane lost lift; both student and instructor bought the farm."

Something snapped in Art. He gave himself one night to make sure he didn't change his mind, but the next morning he didn't don his orange flight suit. With newly shined shoes, he entered the base in dress khakis and DORed.

❖

A week later he went in for the mandatory exit interview in the base captain's spacious corner office. The tall four-striper silently thumbed through a folder that Art suspected was his service record.

"I see you did pretty well in college, Ensign Anthony. What was your major?"

He couldn't believe the size of the Captain's desk. Fifteen feet long, easy. "English, sir."

The Captain leaned back in his swivel chair. "I'm not surprised. You're the fourth English major to drop out recently. Almost half my DORs. I'm sending word back for them not to send another one down here." He sat up ramrod straight in his chair and shut the folder with a thump.

"Dismissed, *Mister* Anthony."

Too Pooped to Pop
By Lucy Ann Murray

LET ME BE CLEAR: I *love* Home and Garden TV (HGTV), but I am trying to cure my addiction to it without resorting to a twelve-step program. Why? It stirs discontent in the hearts of Americans and makes us feel like outdated losers. The channel draws us in and brainwashes us into eying the corners of our homes with fresh HGTV-inspired disgust. The walls are too drab. The appliances, though in perfect working order, are outdated and need to be replaced with cold, industrial stainless steel. You remodeled your kitchen counters with tile in the '80s? Yank them out! A kitchen without granite is like a bathroom without a toilet. They say it's all about resale value. Do I care? The only way I'll leave my nest is in a pine box.

Show hosts take us into nicely adorned homes and shake their heads with revulsion as they cross the thresholds. "What a mess," they say.

I must be clueless, because I admire the traditional landscape painting hung over a sofa. They replace it with what looks like a contemporary interpretation of a salami that ingested the color palette.

Members of the design team shield their eyes from the disaster found in every room. Not one single person in America knows how to arrange furniture. "Where's the crown molding?" they ask. Once desirable wall-to-wall carpeting is now considered a disease magnet. Who knew a person could contract bubonic plague from sitting on plush rugs?

Paneled walls induce gasps. "OMG," they roar, "right out of the '70s—looks like grandma's house!" Heaven help those with the bad taste to hang wallpaper picturing fruits and veggies in their kitchens or those who lacked the wisdom to remove it. These hosts have zero tolerance for clutter. If they had their way, toys and the children who play with them would be stored in the garage and their parents sterilized.

I watched an HGTV designer paint a couple's bedroom walls blacker than charred steak to replace the existing ho-hum cream color. *Seriously*? The goal was to provide the couple a romantic hideaway. Sure, if they could find each other in the dark. Next, he painted the family room bright red with red, white, and black accessories. It resembled a creepy 19th century bordello a cowboy might patronize. If I had to live in such rooms, I'd start dressing like a hooker. The homeowners came in for the reveal and shrieked with delight. Did they pay these poor souls—who now had to live in a whorehouse—to pretend they liked this mess? And who would be attracted to this house if they did want to sell it?

The hosts often contradict one other, especially when it comes to colors. One show tells us to paint at least one wall of a room with bright colors—especially red—to make it "pop." The word "pop" is central to HGTV lingo. Recently, one homeowner painted all of her walls with intense primary colors. Boy, did they pop! It was a bright idea on steroids. She had watched too much HGTV, popping as advised. But when she wanted to sell the home, the host spoke with a forked tongue. "No, no, these walls will send any potential homebuyer *running* to the next open house." The team repainted all rooms a sedate off-white. What a bunch of hypocrites! Are we supposed to pop, or not?

Unfortunately, I too was sucked into the HGTV remodeling vortex. I mimicked the hosts like a parrot with my blabbering about upgrading. The brainwashing was complete last year when I spent thousands of dollars trying to live up to HGTV's standard of what an American home should look like. I plastered walls to give them a Tuscan village effect and painted one wall a darker color in an attempt to make—I confess—the sliding glass door to the patio "pop." To gain curb appeal, I took out the ancient, cracked concrete driveway and installed pavers. I stood on the curb waiting for accolades from my neighbors. Ashamed to have dinner guests see my 1959 Formica kitchen countertops, I replaced them along with the sink and fixtures. On a roll, I tore out the old tiled bathroom. All were HGTV-sanctioned improvements. Now I sit here, broke, waiting for all of it to go out of style. And it will.

My parents lived their entire lives and never remodeled one single thing. My mother's 1936 Servel refrigerator was held together with wire and kept ice cream in a semi-liquid state, but she said it was perfectly good and refused to part with it. Depression-era folks may have gone too far in the other direction, but today we HGTV viewers are becoming fashion addicts and being led like lambs to insolvency. Not to mention—with the exception of some weird HGTV decorating ideas like the above-noted whorehouse—most of us are now living in high-priced "clone" houses complete with crown molding, granite countertops, hardwood floors, stainless steel appliances and at least one wall that "pops"— just like everyone else on the block. And we think we're unique?

So I've decided to stop. All design teams are banned from my viewing lineup. Sure, I have rooms that HGTV would love for me to rip up and remodel. There is no end to it. But I'm not going there. What is remodeled today will be outdated tomorrow. I recently read an article titled, *Granite: On the Way Out!* I knew it.

So why bother? If I wait a few years, what is *out* will be *in*—and what I just spent thousands on bringing *in*—will be *out*. Well, I'm done! Besides, I'm too pooped to *pop*!

Rest in Peace
By Ann Foster

MARCIE MISSED THE 5:30 BUS and was forced to make a decision. Walk or wait for the 6:30. She could hear Bob Dombrowski's snide laughter in the boss's office, so the logical choice was to walk. Miracle Cord Mattress Company was not in the best neighborhood, but if she hurried, there was light enough to make it home before dark. She would have to take the short way past the old Saint Sebastian Cemetery, founded when the first of the city fathers had settled on the swampy bottom lands of the Yavupai River. The ancient trees and dark grave markers haunted her imagination.

To wait around at the office meant putting up with the antics of the big Dumb-kowski. He knew she hated his attention, which seemed to egg him on. *Marcie, Marcie, two by four.* She could hear his sing-song mocking. No, she would walk.

She slipped out of the Miracle Cord Mattress Company offices, making sure Bob Dombrowski didn't see her, and walked toward the corner of General Grant and Chestnut.

Miracle Cord had been a blissful haven until Bob, the uber-salesman, had been hired. Marcie had not only made a comfortable niche for herself, she had made friends.

The owner, Dave Chambers, recruited Marcie to fill in when a winter flu outbreak left the line seriously understaffed. In the space of an hour, the line manager had trained her on the binding machine and what to do if the binding twisted. With one twisting disaster behind her, Marcie determined that the best way to succeed would be to prevent the twist. By the end of the shift, she was confident and capable and no longer slowed the line. The line manager praised her work and let Dave know that her presence insured that orders were filled on time.

After that, Marcie would occasionally visit the line on her break to watch and learn how the other machines worked. The cutters, binders, and buttoners soon depended on her to cover for them if they needed to leave the line for any length of time. It was a noisy place; communications on the line were usually raucous and frequently profane, but there she took plenty of teasing without the fear or revulsion she felt around Bob. A tease from the buttoner one day would turn into a request for help the next, followed by sincere thanks. This was not a pattern she experienced with Bob.

One afternoon, Dave Chambers overheard Bob say "We must be having an earthquake" when Marcie walked by.

"Lay off the girl," Dave said. Marcie was grateful but hurried by, cheeks aflame, pretending not to hear. A hundred times, she tried to work up the courage to go to Dave and let him know that the teasing continued unabated. Bob had just gotten sneakier. But she couldn't follow through. Everyone knew that Bob had saved the company. The company was barely afloat till The Great Dombrowski came on board. Now orders exceeded their capacity and Dave was looking for a bigger facility. Everyone was thrilled. *Almost* everyone.

Clouds had rolled in by the time she reached the corner and the leafless elms in the cemetery rattled and swayed. Maybe this wasn't such a good idea, after all. She *could* cross the street and avoid being in such close proximity to Saint Sebastian, but that meant walking past pimps, porn shops, bars, and the stinky basement boxing gym, aptly named The Sweat Shop. Though The Sweat Shop was housed in a basement, it had high, street-level windows and Marcie was sure the men bashing the leather bags and each other could look up her dress as she passed.

The only good thing on the block was a no-kill Humane Society branch that took in the strays of the neighborhood. Marcie liked to imagine who each of the pathetic little creatures had belonged to. The battered little Boston terrier looked like one of the boxers she had seen several times popping down the steps to the barred basement entrance.

The black tomcat with the perpetually flattened ears would have come from the pimp. In the spring, the Humane Society window was full of an odd assortment of kittens. They were white and black and brown and calico, striped, spotted, solid. Not one looked like another—like the people of the neighborhood.

Marcie would have liked a kitten. Even the evil-looking tom would have been welcome. Too bad about the no-cats-allowed rule at her apartment building.

She dawdled, indecisive. Two men standing in front of the bar were staring at her. Now she wished she had waited for the 6:30 bus. She had to move. Saint Sebastian's, she decided. Tucking her purse tightly under one arm, she looked both ways and crossed. The sidewalk on this side was perpetually shaded and sticky with sap. At least in the shadows, she would be less visible to the men watching.

The cemetery was bounded by a high brick wall, broken mid-block by ornamental iron gates, always open. Angel statuary could be seen through the gate. Angels must have been in vogue when the cemetery was built. Most were quite beautiful, sculpted with graceful, flowing robes and outstretched wings. One, however, was made of polished black stone, granite perhaps, and the expression on its upturned face was angry. Marcie wished she had the courage to walk through the gates and right up to the black angel.

Past the gate, ivy from inside the cemetery draped over the brick wall. It too was black, cursed with a waxy, foul-smelling fungus. She moved to the curb to avoid contamination.

As Marcie approached the end of the block, she glanced back over her shoulder. Four or five men now grouped themselves in the doorway of the bar. Dusk had fallen and all Marcie could see were their silhouettes. They did not seem to notice her. That was good. Someone had turned on the jukebox. Through the open door, she could hear Chuck Berry singing "Roll Over Beethoven." That might have been fun—sit at a bar, have a beer, and put money in a jukebox. She would play something romantic, maybe "Yesterday." Paul was still dreamy, still looked like a kid.

A shout from the door of the bar startled her. The men loitering at the entrance scattered to the street as a man was hurled out onto the sidewalk. Marcie retreated to the shadows near the fence and watched. A giant emerged, silhouetted against the light. The fallen man attempted to get his feet under him, only to be flattened by a vicious kick. The men at the curb laughed and commented, their voices high pitched. The fallen man struggled to his feet and reeled off down the sidewalk.

The wind was at Marcie's back, shoving her forward. She wrapped her long cardigan tightly around her shoulders and scurried on. At the corner of Peterson Boulevard, she crossed into the safety of the strip mall. Kroger's was brightly lit, a haven. She stopped in and bought dinner—a rotisserie chicken and a quart of potato salad. From here, it was an easy down hill.

As she stepped out of the light into the encroaching darkness, a familiar two-toned Ford Crown Victoria eased out of a parking spot and came parallel with her. The driver's window silently recessed. "Hey, Marcie," a soft voice sang. "You need a lift?"

She shook her head, gripping her bags to her chest.

"Come on, girl. I don't bite."

"No, I don't need a ride." She shook her head again and hurried down the mall. The car paced her.

"What's the matter? I'm not good enough for you? You being stuck up, or just playing hard to get?"

"I don't need a ride, Bob." Marcie forced herself to speak clearly. "Thank you, but no." She wondered if she should go back to the store when she heard a voice behind her.

"Mister, the lady said no." Marcie turned to see a kid in a Kroger shirt and apron approaching Bob's car.

"Marcie! You got a boyfriend," Bob taunted.

As the kid approached Bob's car, he reached into his pocket. Bob reacted by rolling up his window and pulling away from the curb, but another car blocked his way. Marcie, too, reacted by drawing back, but the kid was holding a cell phone. She breathed a sigh.

161

"I'm calling security," the kid shouted at Bob. "We have your license plate number now, and if . . ." The temporary jam cleared and Bob pulled away with a screech of tires. The kid back-pedaled to the curb, throwing the retreating car a one-finger salute.

"Thank you," Marcie said.

"No problem. I heard him call you Marcie. That your name?"

"Yes." Marcie continued to clutch her grocery bags as a shield.

"I'm Malcolm. I know you from somewhere." He paused, thinking. "Yeah! I seen you at the shelter up the street, looking in the window."

"You were at the shelter?" Marcie relaxed her arms.

"Yeah, I work a split shift on Tuesday and Thursday, so I volunteer there, rather than go home. You like animals?"

"I do, yes."

"You should stop in sometime. Pick out a kitten or puppy. We have lots of critters needing good homes."

Marcie sighed. "I can't have a pet in my apartment house."

"I know how that goes." Malcolm nodded. "It's the same for me. It's one of the reasons I work there." He paused, smiling. "Listen, I gotta get back to work. Even if you can't adopt, you should stop in. It's a great place to volunteer and hang out with the animals and the staff. Think about it, okay?"

"Oh, that sounds, well, nice. Thanks for letting me know and thanks again for—you know—Bob."

"Hey, my pleasure." Malcolm gave her a wave and trotted back to the front of the store. Marcie watched him till the sliding doors whooshed open like wings and he disappeared inside.

The Eyes Have It
By Lisa Meltzer Penn

I DON'T KNOW HOW TO TELL YOU THIS. But we draw dangerously near the day when I will have no more say over you. And it is time. It's past all time. Even as I speak I feel myself weakening.

Brace yourself, my rosebud. What you need to know is this: Your name is not your name. Your skin is not your skin. The tiny fine hairs—perhaps. The beauty marks—maybe. But never the skin. And your body? It is not yours.

The eyes, however, the doorway through which everything enters, are entirely yours. They are all that you truly possess.

After you protest, after you reject what I am telling you, you will search. With those smoldering, angry eyes you will try to trace yourself back as fiercely as you deny what has come before. You will search as far as you can for your real name and your real skin. Tear everything apart, little thorny one. They are nowhere here, I assure you.

Away from this hidden place, away from we who have played the role of family and supporters to perfection, away from your brother who has loved you more sincerely than anyone. You might come back to him someday. Though I doubt it. Likely he wouldn't know you next time around. I fear you will be gone for good. And, my hollyhock, there's no more good here for you.

But that is your right and prerogative. Just remember: You will be walking on feet and legs that are not yours. Touching with hands you do not own. They were never yours to hold or keep. Long ago, when you were a tiny thing, I gripped your fingers and led you away from your name. Already then I knew.

You chide me, glare at me. You don't believe me, do you, child?

But you will.

Because I will bring you to your knees, my cloudlet, my little bee. I will bring you down on those knees that do not belong to you. They were yielded, but not willingly, not to keep. Yes, you were taken. Yes, you were changed and given to me. But the thief was one and the same with you, my slender stinging nettle. Harmer and healer joined. You stole when no one was looking. You'll say we tricked you, enchanted you here, chained you to this life, but I know better. We protected you, black-eyed Susan turning toward the sun.

And I have had your back. It was never yours.

One last time, my changeling, I run the edge of my finger along your cheek and the outline of your throat. If I must, I will silence the fat pink muscle in your mouth. But I must not. There are rules to follow. I was commanded, as were you.

The sun is setting. Look what I've prepared. Beer brewed in pale eggshells. A half-shell of stew. You've always been insatiable. Will you have these or simply laugh at their absurdity? Will you proclaim yourself older than the hills or still just fifteen years of age?

You follow my movements, daughter, with those burning, watchful eyes that I cannot have. They are truly yours. To be fair, you had to find your way here somehow. Well, let those eyes see. Let their sight fall upon every moment that is still lit. I pick up an eggshell cup myself and drink the liquid down. I can't wait for your response. I drink another and another, each no more than a swallow.

You should know, my milk thistle, my pussy willow: You own everything that comes through your eyes. All the light and images they absorb are sent to the brain, captured and changed into you. Still life, stop-motion, flashes of movement, all of it, the images burned in. What you see overrides even smell and touch, the deepest, most primordial senses from as far back as can be traveled. I should know. I've been there. Do you remember yet?

The eyes are a conduit to the soul, a soul you do not own. But don't worry, my teacup, my buttercup, my poppy, neither do I, nor anyone else. Your secret is safe with me.

Safer than you yourself will be, when this spell of protection is broken and all reverts to its former state. Then what changeling twin might seek her way backwards to this place? No, whom do I think I am fooling? Surely it is too late for that.

The eyes are the rulers. If you did not have eyes, the other senses—touch, smell, taste, sound—might come forward to take the throne and crown. Perhaps you still could accomplish your search then, dear borrower of body. Except, of course, that without your eyes and what they capture behind the discs of iris, nothing would be left that was yours.

Or am I mistaken? I could be. Perhaps it was only a dream? Don't take all this the wrong way, my rainbow, my love. It was never intended to be any other way.

My wishes blow away on the evening breeze, bits of white fluff carried this direction and that, already beyond my thin grasp. I am growing weaker, losing strength. I am not what I used to be.

You might have the last word after all, my dandelion, my wish, my puff of breath. Spoken with your borrowed, fleshly tongue. Punctuated with your eyes, black as a river.

Author Biographies

Kevin Arnold

Kevin Arnold has published fifty stories and poems in literary magazines such as *Seattle Review* and *Beloit Fiction Journal*. He spent an extraordinary week in Raymond Carver's workshop at Centrum in 1982. Serving as president of the Poetry Center San Jose from 2001 to 2013, he earned his MFA from San Jose State University in 2007 and was a founder of and teaches at Gold Rush Writers. Kevin is tickled that the San Francisco/Peninsula Writers, a branch of the California Writers Club, named him Writer of the Year for 2014.

Sue Barizon

Sue Barizon, the daughter of immigrant parents, was born in San Francisco and raised in San Mateo. She writes mostly memoir about life's lessons learned growing up in mid-century suburbia. She began writing as a means to "quiet the buzzing in my head left by the Jiminy Cricket moments of my youth." Two of her short stories, "The Garbageman's Daughter" and "Off Guard" have been published in *Fault Zone* anthologies. She was awarded 2013 Writer of the Year Award by the San Francisco/Peninsula Writers, a branch of the California Writers Club. She serves as assistant director for the San Mateo County Fair.

Jo Carpignano

Jo Carpignano is a retired educator and school psychologist now residing in San Mateo. She enjoys writing and her favorite hobby is entering writing contests. In 2013, she won the title of Senior Poet Laureate at the national level. In 2012, she won the California Senior Poet Laureate title and was runner up in 2011. She wrote a biography about her immigrant mother and enjoys writing personal essays, poetry, and short stories. She is actively involved with Crystal Springs Writers as well as San

Francisco/Peninsula Writers, a branch of the California
Writers Club.

Dorcas Cheng-Tozun

Dorcas Cheng-Tozun is a writer, blogger, and editor whose
personal essays and short stories have been published in Hong
Kong, the UK, and the US. Prior to becoming a full-time writer,
Dorcas spent more than ten years managing corporate
communications and development projects with nonprofits,
government agencies, and social enterprises in the US and
abroad. A full-length memoir about her time in Shenzhen is in
the works. Follow her at www.chengtozun.com or on Twitter
@dorcas_ct.

Emily Eddins

Emily Eddins has been a professional writer for twenty years.
Her career includes time spent as a speechwriter, a journalist,
and an editor. She holds a BA from Vanderbilt University and
an MA from Georgetown University and has studied creative
writing at both Georgetown University and Stanford
University. Her poetry and nonfiction have appeared in
publications such as *The Willow Review*, *The Louisville Review*,
The Toad Suck Review, *Forge*, *RiversEdge*, *The Cape Rock*, and
others. Fun fact: she is named after Emily Dickinson.

Ann Foster

Ann Foster is the 2011 recipient of the Jack London Award
from San Francisco/Peninsula Writers, a branch of the
California Writers Club and winner of the 2011 Foster City
Writing Contest, personal essay division. Ann writes fiction
and narrative non-fiction and her work is published in *The
Sand Hill Review*; *Fault Zone: Words from the Edge*; *Fault Zone:
Stepping up to the Edge*; and *Fault Zone: Over the Edge*. She is
now working on a novel set in post-civil war Missouri and
Texas.

Darlene Frank

Darlene Frank is a writer, editor, and creativity coach who helps writers gain creative confidence and fulfill their artistic vision and dreams. She works with nonfiction authors especially in the self-help and memoir genres and with writers who have undergone a radical life transformation and want to create art from that experience. Darlene has written two business books and teaches workshops on how to navigate the writer's journey. Her stories have been published in four prior issues of *Fault Zone* and the anthology *The Times They Were A-Changing: Women Remember the '60s and '70s* (She Writes Press, 2013). Learn more at www.DarleneFrankWriting.com.

James Hanna

James Hanna roamed Australia for seven years before settling on a career in criminal justice. He spent twenty years as a counselor in the Indiana Department of Corrections and has recently retired from the San Francisco Probation Department, where he was assigned to a domestic violence and stalking unit. James' short stories have appeared in *Old Crow Review*, *Edge City Review*, *Eclipse*, *Fault Zone*, *The California Writers Club Literary Review*, *Red Savina Review*, *The Literary Review*, *Empty Sink Publishing*, *Zymbol*, and *The Sand Hill Review* (where he was formerly the fiction editor). Three of his stories were nominated for the Pushcart Prize. James' novel, *The Siege*, which depicts a hostage standoff in a penal facility, is available on Amazon Kindle. His novella, *Call Me Pomeroy*, will be published in March 2015 through Sand Hill Review Press.

Karen Hartley

Karen writes stories, poetry, and memoir. Her story "Beach House" is published in the July 2012 issue of the *Sand Hill Review* and "Graveside Angel" appears in *Carry the Light*, the 2013 anthology of the San Mateo County Fair. A dual member of South Bay Writers, Karen's stories and poems appear regularly in their *Writers Talk* newsletter. She facilitates a mixed-genre critique group twice a month. Contact her at Sew1Machin@aol.com.

Laurel Anne Hill

Laurel Anne Hill joined the California Writers Club in 1999. KOMENAR Publishing released her award-winning novel, *Heroes Arise*, in 2007. Two dozen of her science fiction and fantasy short stories have appeared in a variety of publications, most recently in the anthologies *How Beer Saved the World*, *A Bard in the Hand*, *Horrible Disasters*, *Fault Zone*, and *Shanghai Steam*, a steampunk-wuxia collection. In April 2013, *Shanghai Steam* was nominated for an Aurora Award in Canada. Visit Laurel's website and podcast at www.laurelannehill.com.

Diane Jacobson

As any true Montana girl would, Diane Jacobson is weathering the Bay Area with an arsenal of fish stories to tell, a Leatherman tool in her purse, and a row of boots in her closet. She lives in San Carlos with her husband, son, and dog, where she is at work on short fiction and a novel.

Amy Kelm

Amy Kelm is rediscovering her passion for creative writing after a long hiatus. A former marketing executive, she is now blessed to spend her days volunteering and soaking up all the living she can with her husband and two growing children. When not writing, she can be found picking socks up off the floor and tormenting her children with blended vegetable smoothies. Her work has appeared previously in *Fault Zone: Over The Edge*. She lives in San Mateo County.

Maurine Killough

Maurine is inspired by life stories of human frailty and the existential experience of being alive. She believes "poetry bridges the material world to the dream world, helping us to stay in touch with the dream—the creative and spiritual part of being alive." Her poems have appeared in several publications including the online *Loch Raven Review* and *Poems from Conflicted Hearts*, by Tayen Lane. She is a two-time first place winner for free-form poetry at the San Mateo County Fair and has published one book of poems, *Underseams*. Her poetry blog, iwritemyself.wordpress.com, features local artists and beyond. Please visit!

Bardi Rosman Koodrin

Bardi Rosman Koodrin began writing her first novel in 1990 and hasn't stopped since. She's now on novel number four, plus she's written more than seventy short stories, numerous articles, and online columns. She is the Literary Director of the Fine Arts Galleria at the San Mateo County Fair, giving writers a presence and a voice, and is a board member of the San Francisco/Peninsula Writers, a branch of the California Writers Club. After championing the club motto *Writers Helping Writers* for years, she was thrilled to win her first international literary prize for a personal essay, "Zazen in the Zendo," which was also published in the 2014 anthology *Fault Zone: Shift*. Her advice is to keep writing and never give up!

Eileen Malone

Eileen Malone lives in the coastal fog surrounded by Daly City and Colma. Her written works have appeared in over 500 literary journals and anthologies, and she has published one award-winning poetry collection, one book-length poetry collection, and one non-fiction book. She founded and directs the Soul-Making Keats Literary Competition. She is the winner of the Fault Zone Contest for 2015.

Elise Frances Miller

Elise Frances Miller's novel, *A Time to Cast Away Stones* (Sand Hill Review Press, 2012), emerged from her experiences in Berkeley and Paris in 1968. Her memoir, "My People's Park," won second prize for prose in *The Times They Were A-Changing: Women Remember the '60s and '70s* (She Writes Press, 2013). She began her writing career as an art critic and reviewer, and her short stories have appeared in *The Sand Hill Review*, for which she served as guest fiction editor in 2008, and in two previous *Fault Zone* publications. She is membership chair for the San Francisco/Peninsula Writers, a branch of the California Writers Club. Visit her at www.elisefmiller.com.

Diane Lee Moomey

Diane grew up around the Great Lakes, and since then has lived and wandered around the US and Canada. Now she dips her gardener's hands in California dirt. Her poetry and short prose have appeared, or are scheduled to appear soon, in *Red Wheelbarrow*, *Glass: a Journal of Poetry*, the *Fault Zone* anthologies, *No Ordinary Language* (the Willow Glen Poetry Project anthology), *The Sand Hill Review*, *Not Somewhere Else But Here*, (Sundress Publications) and *Writing For Our Lives*. Day'sEye Press and Studios published her book *Silk Road, Iron Bird* in 2011 and *...Place...* in 2010. *Figure in a Landscape*, a collection of new poetry, is scheduled to appear in late 2014. To read more, please visit www.dianeleemoomeywrites.com.

Lucy Ann Murray

Lucy Ann Murray is a local artist, crafter, and freelance writer. She has more than one hundred published pieces in a variety of genres, including essay, biography, history, poetry, and fiction. Her writing has appeared in local and national publications and in ten anthologies, including all four *Fault Zone* anthologies. She has won seven writing awards. She has been a correspondent for a Chicago-based publication for the last fifteen years. She currently writes a monthly newsletter for The Family Tree, an auxiliary of Peninsula Family Services. She lives in Belmont with her husband Jim, her best friend and golf partner.

Linda Okerlund

Linda Okerlund lives and works on the San Francisco Peninsula. Work takes her through much of California and the desert southwest, where she mines her experiences and memories of the Santa Clara Valley before it became Silicon into her essays and fiction.

Lisa Meltzer Penn

Lisa Meltzer Penn has contributed short stories, prose poetry, and novel excerpts to multiple *Fault Zone* anthologies. Her work also appears in the *Sand Hill Review XII*, *Best of the Sand Hill Review*, *Travelers' Tales: Spain*, *Travelers' Tales: San Francisco*, *Transfer Magazine* and *The Cupboard*. With an extensive background in New York publishing, Lisa has worked hands-on with authors on both coasts for thirty years, and served as founding editor of the *Fault Zone* series. She now lives with her husband, two children, and dog on the Peninsula.

Frank A. Saunders

Frank A. Saunders writes poetry, fiction, scientific articles, and music, most recently the portfolio *A Scent of Tea*. He lives in Foster City with his wife, Barbara, and daughter, Andrea. He has taught physiological psychology at San Francisco State University and is a licensed clinical neuropsychologist. Visit his website at www.frankasaunders.com.

Martha Clark Scala

Martha Clark Scala writes poetry when she isn't gardening, rooting for the San Francisco Giants, counseling adults, grieving many losses, or buying groceries. Her work can also be found in *Porter Gulch Review*, *Poetry Now*, the *California Writers Club Literary Review* and at her website, www.mcscala.com.

Ellen Six

Ellen Six is an adjunct associate professor at Dominican University in San Rafael, California. She is currently writing a memoir of her experiences teaching in Lithuania after the fall of Communism. She has won awards in writing from the San Mateo County fair in the Memoir and Immigrant Experience categories. She is published in volumes 1, 2, and 3 of *Carry the Light* and in *Tuxedo Lit*, a literary journal of Dominican University. She presented a workshop on the Spiritual Seasons of Life at the 2014 Dr. Oz Create Your Future Health Summit. This event focused on the whole person, body, mind, and spirit.

Eve Visconti

Eve Visconti has been writing all her life, coming from a family of writers and editors. She's been published in the *North American Review of Literature*, two anthologies—including *Fault Zone: Words from the Edge*—in several newspapers, and on the Internet.

Wendy Walter

Wendy loves world building, even more than chocolate. Her passion for restructuring environments began in school, when interior architecture first tweaked her interest. But after years of designing office buildings, she became disillusioned with the constraints of reality. So she picked up her pencil and started dreaming up her own quirky worlds. She uses stories and illustrations to usher anyone who is interested through them. Wendy has published two books and is the editor of the *Sand Hill Review*, a literary anthology. She lives near San Francisco with her husband, daughters, tabby cat, and border collie.

Ollie Mae Trost Welch

Ollie Mae Trost Welch has a degree in creative writing and English literature from San Francisco State University. She is a writer of fiction, non-fiction, poems, and plays. She is currently busy collecting and editing her five novellas under the title *The Dirt Road Leads to Heaven*. Her memoir is published under the title *Coming of Age in the Ozarks*. One of her plays was performed at Dominican University in the fall of 2012.

Fault Zone Contest Winners

First Place
Eileen Malone, "Back Story of the Back Road"

Second Place
Doug Fortier, "Guilty by Association"

Third Place
Carole Taub, "Traveling Grannie"

Finalists:
Madeline McEwen, "Cry Baby Bunting"
V.E. Duncan, "Julian"
Norma Armon, "My Knight in Black"
Katie Burke, "Oni's Dearest Husband"
Piotr Cymbalski, "A Cat, and a Teakettle"
Joseph Dworetsky, "At the DMV"
John Trout, "Ebb and Flow"

Every year the San Francisco/Peninsula Writers, a branch of the California Writers Club, sponsors a short story contest for non-members. Check our website for details.
www.cwc-peninsula.org

www.ingramcontent.com/pod-product-compliance
Lightning Source LLC
Chambersburg PA
CBHW021154130626
46554CB00005B/1805